Totally Bound Publishing books by Amber Malloy

Spies R Us
Spies R Us
Kill Shot

Perfect Stats
Winning Her
Hard Knox

Perfect Stats

HARD KNOX

AMBER MALLOY

Hard Knox
ISBN # 978-1-83943-898-1
©Copyright Amber Malloy 2020
Cover Art by Louisa Maggio ©Copyright June 2020
Interior text design by Claire Siemaszkiewicz
Totally Bound Publishing

This is a work of fiction. All characters, places and events are from the author's imagination and should not be confused with fact. Any resemblance to persons, living or dead, events or places is purely coincidental.

All rights reserved. No part of this publication may be reproduced in any material form, whether by printing, photocopying, scanning or otherwise without the written permission of the publisher, Totally Bound Publishing.

Applications should be addressed in the first instance, in writing, to Totally Bound Publishing. Unauthorised or restricted acts in relation to this publication may result in civil proceedings and/or criminal prosecution.

The author and illustrator have asserted their respective rights under the Copyright Designs and Patents Acts 1988 (as amended) to be identified as the author of this book and illustrator of the artwork.

Published in 2020 by Totally Bound Publishing, United Kingdom.

No part of this book may be reproduced, scanned, or distributed in any printed or electronic form without permission. Please do not participate in or encourage piracy of copyrighted materials in violation of the authors' rights. Purchase only authorised copies.

Totally Bound Publishing is an imprint of Totally Entwined Group Limited.

If you purchased this book without a cover you should be aware that this book is stolen property. It was reported as "unsold and destroyed" to the publisher and neither the author nor the publisher has received any payment for this "stripped book".

HARD KNOX

Dedication

To the woman who used to make me read
Stephen King to her on long drives.
Thanks, Mom

Prologue

With less than a minute on the clock, Gavin Knox faked right and threw the ball to his running back. His teammate's gravity-defying catch took place in the end zone, resulting in their game-winning touchdown. As the band played the school's fight song, the student body of Michigan Institute of Technology flooded the field.

Letting out a ferocious howl, Knox snatched off his helmet. For the second time in a row his team was headed to the championships. With only one more year left in college, Knox looked forward to the Heisman Trophy Ceremony and a single digit position in the professional draft.

It may have seemed arrogant on his part to assume that he had a right to any of those things, but he had worked his ass off. He had mapped out his whole career since the age of twelve. In his freshman year of high school, Knox had transferred to America from Canada to secure his spot in the pros. He'd then followed it up with enrollment at a Big Ten college.

Intending to get drunk off his ass, Knox scanned the crowd for his best friend, Hawk. On his way past a couple of his teammates, he slapped their heads as he moved closer to the stands — and that was when he saw her. A chocolate-colored honey ran straight at him. Her letterman jacket showcased her body-hugging, tight sweater and perfect tits. Since she was focused on something over her shoulder, Knox felt safe to peruse her banging-ass body without judgment.

However, once she turned those big, almond-shaped eyes in his direction, his whole world came to a sudden and glorious halt. Shiny black curls bounced up and down, framing her heart-shaped face. Simple and utter perfection barreled straight at him.

As she licked her full lips, instant wood clouded his mind. Even if he wanted to, he couldn't seem to stop himself. Fate had other plans. Flashes of what life would be like if he didn't talk to her propelled him into action. Knox reached out to snag her around the waist, bringing the beauty inches from his mug.

"Where did you come from?" he asked her.

Confusion shuttled across her stunning face before she tilted her head to the side and smiled. "Nowhere."

"So you just fell out of the sky?" It might have sounded lame, but he meant every word of it.

"Technically, you grabbed me. So, what happened here?" She checked out the field. "Did you win something big?"

"If the answer's 'you', then sure." As he looked into her eyes, he almost forgot the last few minutes of his life.

"Do you mind?" She glanced down at the ground. "The air's kind of thin up here in Giantsville."

Though he was reluctant to let her go, he set her down.

"So, what...? Are you like the main guy?" she asked, looking totally serious.

Knox laughed. He couldn't help it. Obviously she didn't care about football. "Something like that."

"Which makes you a supastar, right?"

Positive that she didn't have a bra on under her soft, cream-colored sweater, he desperately wanted to feel her body against his one more time.

"Are you going to tell me your name?" he asked abruptly. She glanced over her shoulder at something. For a split second he wondered if she had a boyfriend, but, truthfully, he didn't care.

"And make it easy for you? No, but" — she raised onto her tiptoes and Knox leaned down to meet her halfway — "dream about me, okay? Then just maybe..." The warmth of her candy-scented breath heated his cheek.

Tempted to tip his head down a little farther to intercept her lips, he froze and hit the dreaded blue screen.

"Hey, man, congrat-u-fucking-lations!" His friend Hawk grabbed him in a big bear hug. When the melody of her laughter kicked him into gear, he realized that the beauty had disappeared.

Knox searched the crowd but couldn't find her. "Where did she go?" he asked.

"Who? What the hell are you talking about? I didn't see anybody."

Positive that she'd given him a hint to her name, he ran through the possibilities in his head.

"The press wants to talk to you. Then we're going out to celebrate." Hawk patted him on the back and led him toward the locker room. Still shell-shocked by his encounter with the hottest girl he had ever laid eyes on, he reluctantly followed his friend.

* * * *

Once they had been deemed champions for the second year running, Knox only had to worry about finals, which were right around the corner. He rested on his ability to memorize things quickly. In other words, he planned to coast. Not in the least bit worried about his grades, he hit the coffee shop in the quad.

"Hard Knox!"

He nodded at a table full of people he didn't know. Winners were always recognizable on campus. In his first year, no one had even known his name. Pretty sure some of his teammates were at the *Half Full Coffee Shop*, he skimmed the busy hub.

When he saw her, every nerve in his body rejoiced. "You!" Knox stumbled over a few coeds who were unlucky enough to litter his path to her.

"Hey, jerk!" someone called.

"So-o-ory," he offered, without being sorry at all.

They mocked him over his Canadian dialect slip-up and he repeated his apology, this time making an attempt at sincerity as well as better pronunciation.

In his free time, he had searched for the girl who'd run into him at the playoffs. After a while, he'd convinced himself that there was no way she existed on this worldly plane. With only one thing on his mind, he hurried to intercept his real-life hallucination.

"Supastar!" she cried with a teasing tone. "Don't tell me you won something else."

Tight jeans, camo jacket and a tank with a bra. Dammit, he groused in his head. "If it's not you, then the answer's no."

"Ah-h-h."

"Ni-i-i-ice, white boy. We like this one," someone commented from a table full of chicks who stared at him with different degrees of expression, which ranged from mocking to flat-out humor.

"Gavin, but everyone calls me Knox," he introduced himself. "And you are?"

"Ah, come on now. No fair… You stumbled on to me. You didn't really look."

"What?" he asked, shocked. Knox never got turned down. This wasn't a hard-to-get act she was putting on, but it was something else that he couldn't figure out.

"Ladies," she asked her friends, "does the campus coffee shop count?"

"No!" everyone yelled.

"Hey, I thought you were on my side," he muttered.

"For some reason, they all think that," someone muttered. All the chicks laughed at his expense.

"One more time, Supastar—and with feeling," his dream girl said, her eyes sparkling with humor. "Then you can get a name."

"MIT Campus has over forty-three thousand students. Do you actually think this is a one-off? Let me guess… You do this a lot." The corners of her lips twitched into a devastatingly sexy smirk. He turned to her table of friends. "How many guys get an actual name?"

"So far"—one girl with a buzz haircut counted on her hand, then switched to the next—"none." The table laughed, a hard 'don't give a shit' rip. It plainly expressed that none of them cared if they hurt his feelings or not.

"Then when I do really, really look for you and succeed, I want a name and a date."

"*When?*" she repeated his words before she bit her lower lip. "The confidence on you, Supastar…"

"And no bullshit coffee or lunch. I'm talking a real date."

"O-o-oh, girl, I like this one," her friend said.

As she held out her hand, that teasing smile never left her face. He wanted to snatch her to his chest and kiss her breathless. Needless to say, his six-foot-six frame wouldn't save him from her bodyguards, who hadn't taken their eyes off him from the minute he had shown up.

Knox settled for the slight touch of her hand and shook it. "Deal."

* * * *

Instead of studying for finals, he had spent the last two weeks searching for phantom hot girl. Almost positive he could skate on an eighty in his Financial Accounting and Reporting course, he hadn't bothered to pick up a book.

He got a text from Hawk.

Where are you?

Knox answered.

Stalking my dream girl.

Then he erased it before it was sent. His friend would think he was crazy. Knox put his phone back into his pocket and took out a fifty-dollar bill.

"They're in the last bay down the hall," the security guard who had called him said.

Knox slapped the bill into the man's palm on his way past. Describing Hot Girl to people had become a painful endeavor that he felt had equipped him to teach as a subject for an entire semester. Confessing that he hadn't known one thing about her had become downright embarrassing. Sadly, it had turned into a nut-slamming experience when he explained this to black people.

After they understood that he was indeed serious, their amusement had immediately switched to pity. Knox had a feeling that even if they had known, they still wouldn't have told him. Hot Girl had no social media of any sort.

He'd asked a couple of guys on the team, but that hadn't gotten anywhere. Most of them lived in sports housing. Unless she traveled in their circle, Hot Girl had managed to ghost an entire university. Then it had occurred to him that her friends had worn sorority jackets. Once he'd started with that thin thread of evidence, it had led him to the university pool. Every week the ladies would sneak into the building. Since most of them swam naked, the guards allowed it and kept tabs on them over the monitors.

Leaning against the brick wall, Knox played with his phone. A half-hour later, the girl of his dreams walked out of the women's locker room.

"Supastar!" she cried. Her wet hair made her appear vulnerable and sweet, while her dark T-shirt molded to her skin. He had to imagine practice on a hot summer day to control a woody from springing up and embarrassing him. "How did you find me?"

"Tenacity." He kicked off the wall. "Name."

"Remy."

Of course she was named after a stiff drink. "Full name?"

"We're not there yet." She chuckled. "Where do you want to meet?"

"Are you kidding me?" Shocked, his mouth fell open. "What happened to the 'pick you up at the door' type of deal?"

"Take it or leave it, Supastar." Remy winked, and her obnoxiously hot, flirtatious act caused his stomach to do cartwheels.

"Had you given me your name already, we could have been over this part by now."

"So-o-o confident." Her whole face lit up.

Down, dick, down, he instructed his cock.

"Are you going?" Eight of her friends gathered at the locker room entrance, waiting for her to answer.

"A deal's a deal," she said.

"Well, all right, white boy."

The ladies favored him with a slow, off-beat clap of congratulations that he happily accepted. Regardless of the sarcastic overtone, Knox took a much-deserved bow.

Chapter One

Six years later

Absorbing the manic energy from the crowd, the Mavericks football team jogged down the hallway leading out to the field. Knox had a load of shit on his mind, but if he wanted to lead his team to victory, he needed to focus.

"We are warriors. We are gladiators. We are *beasts*!" Andre Burnet, their running back, shouted before they took that last step into the stadium. "And if you don't know anything else, you know to get the ball to that fucking superhero." They slapped each other on the head and ran onto the field. The whole first string howled.

Returning his mind back to the task at hand, Knox threw his head back and joined them. "Let's win this mutha fucka!"

And win they did! After they'd stumbled along with a rough first half of the game, the Mavericks had taken control of the ball in the third quarter and scored their city a second Mega Bowl title.

Sweat-soaked, Knox flipped his winning Mega Bowl hat around to face the back and put it on his head. After copious amounts of champagne and confetti had hit the field, key players of the team were now forced to talk to the press before they could party. They sat at the press conference table with the giant trophy placed dead center between the team's starters.

"This is your second consecutive win. What was your team's strategy?" a dude from *SportsNet* asked. Knox couldn't remember his name, but his fresh face rang a bell. Eventually, the grit of the football beat would knock that eager expression straight off his mug.

"Our defense was on point, and once our QB got the ball, it was nothing but T-town," Andre told the reporters.

"Knox, you've had a good season, but your personal life has far surpassed anything you've achieved on the field."

"Look, Artie... I know you were rooting for the Steers, but you got stuck with me," Knox told the old man he'd had a run-in with at his very first Maverick's press conference. Everyone in the room chuckled. Artie had been a thorn in his side ever since.

"No, no... It's just that you've been linked to pop stars and models, but there's no mention of the woman you married in college. And it looks like you are still married to —"

A freight train of panic roared between his ears. He knew that one day it would get out. He had actually counted on it. However, he hadn't thought that this was going to be that day.

"At the time, your father wasn't Canada's prime minster. There's speculation that you needed a green card to stay in the country for the draft."

As everyone waited for his answer, complete silence took over the floor. Artie had always had a hard-on for him and gave him bits of grief from time to time. The old shit must have finally decided to take his big shot before he retired. Instead of allowing the dread of the unknown to settle into his soul, Knox plastered on his most dazzling smile.

"Sorry, Artie. The only quote you're getting from me is that my dance card is full. That's what you old-timers understand as 'I'm not available', right?" His team laughed, which helped break the strange tension in the room. "Other than that, I don't talk about my personal life."

"But we do." Andre grabbed the microphone away from him. "Our boy Bo is currently available, so anyone who doesn't want our handsome quarterback, talk to Easy Breezy over here."

The whole room laughed.

While that tight fist of anxiety punched at his gut, Knox texted two little words on his phone.

Need you.

* * * *

The press had camped outside his Chicago condo for days. Early that morning, he'd had to exit through the dry cleaners that was stationed at the opposite end of the building. Amazed that no one had caught on to that trick, he pressed his luck a little bit more and grabbed a coffee down the street. Hopefully, the excitement over his personal life would end sooner rather than later.

After the promotional tour, he could leave the States in search of Remy.

Knox rode the elevator up to the penthouse. The private one for his suite only worked from the garage. Unfortunately, *TMZ* and *Entertainment Tonight* had posted around-the-clock camera guys at every entrance.

When the cab doors opened to his floor, he found a very serious-looking woman standing in front of his condo. Dripping sweat from his workout, he sighed. Knox took out his earbuds to greet glasses, gray hair and a business suit. The real-life version of Edna E. Mode from *The Incredibles* stared at him.

"Gavin Knox, Doris Petite," she greeted him in a dry tone. "Your father hired me. I'm your fixer."

As he unlocked the door and held it open for her, Knox noted the woman's rigid posture. "Aren't you a couple of days late?" She merely waved her hand at him on her way past. "If I'd known you were coming, I would have picked you up something." He held up his coffee cup.

"Water's fine," she said in a no-nonsense tone.

Knox followed her in to his luxury two-story condo. To curb his love of all things country, he'd made sure to pay for the best view in the city.

Doris walked into his place and set her purse down on his coffee table. "I'm going to get straight to the point. I don't need you to tell me any long, drawn-out story. I just need truthful answers to the questions that I ask. If I feel you're deceptive in any way, I'm out." She handled a couple of his picture frames and souvenirs before placing them back on his shelf.

Given that she wasn't exactly the warm, fuzzy type, Knox figured she must have been good at her job. Letting her explore his condo, he headed to the fridge.

"Is someone here?" Doris crossed his open floor plan toward the guest room. It was tucked away underneath the staircase.

"No." Knox opened the fridge door to grab her a water. The maid only worked once a week and his best friend, Hawk, had an out-of-state game. Since he usually stayed in the spare room, Knox had the place to himself.

When he shut the door, Doris stood directly in front of him. Adding stealthy to his mental resume for her, he passed her the bottle of water. "Considering you're in enough trouble, I would suggest you keep your groupies in check for a while."

"Wow, plural, not singular," a voice he hadn't heard for a while remarked.

As Remy Bell walked into the room, the hard hit of warmth spread through his chest. Wearing nothing but a towel, Remy's huge curls billowed around her gorgeous head. He stared at the woman who held every part of his heart.

"Well, if it isn't Hot Wife," he said, grinning from ear to ear.

"Supastar." She threw him a crazy, sexy smile. "Heard you won a shiny doodad!"

"More like a pretty whatchamacallit," he joked with her as the muted rays of the sun illuminated her cinnamon-colored skin. Knox fought the urge to push the publicist out of his path, but in a few short steps, he planted himself in front of Remy.

"What the entire hell!" Doris screamed. "Nope, nope, nopity-nope-nope... A hooker and a pound of coke— Is that too much to ask?" At an Olympic-style sprint, Doris grabbed her purse. Her sensible shoes tapped against his marble tiles near the foyer. "I don't give a shit who your father is."

Remy jumped from the hard slam of the door, but her smile remained in place. "Is it something I said?"

Ignoring that strange display of weirdness from the fixer, he slipped his arms around her.

When she flinched from his touch, he stopped his advancement inches away from her pouty lips. "What?"

"I had a thing at the airport," she confessed.

"How big?" In an effort not to hurt her, he softened his touch, softly brushing his lips over hers.

"A smidge of a tumble."

Knox's chest tightened in that twisty, churning way that had threatened to consume him in the past. "Did someone assist in this inconsequential fall?" He nipped at her bottom lip.

"Running was involved," she confirmed.

Unable to wait another second, Knox claimed her mouth. He took her lips between his and sucked, tenderly at first. His desire ramped up several notches.

"Hospital," he hissed, hoping he could talk his dick down long enough to grab his keys.

"Clinic." She matched the intensity of his lips. "They don't keep the same type of records."

Knox lingered for a moment longer before pulling away. "Need help getting dressed?"

A slight smirk transformed her angelic face into that sex kitten he loved. "I'm thinking no."

Chapter Two

Remy ran over the menu in search of a vegetarian dish. She'd been meat-free for the past few months but hadn't told Knox...yet. By the way he anxiously bobbed his leg up and down, she assumed this probably wasn't the best time to spring it on him.

"The doctor said you should rest, so why didn't we go straight home?" he wondered aloud.

"That fixer your dad hired changed her mind. Besides, she cleared out this really cool hipster restaurant for us." Completely empty except for a few staff members, the little place had the cutest distressed brick walls. After they found a table that could accommodate Knox's large frame, they waited for Doris to join them.

As Remy continued to scan the menu, she put her hand on his knee to calm his nerves.

"A little higher, baby," he teased.

She glanced at the football hero. Dark brown hair, full lips and a square jaw that God had topped off with the most dazzling blue eyes she had ever seen created the perfect male specimen. Knox straightened his long legs out next to her.

While his white T-shirt stretched across his muscled chest, his jeans covered his amazing everything else. He would have appeared completely relaxed if his restless leg hadn't given him away. Nervous energy seemed to radiate through the beautiful man's entire body. Usually Knox hid his emotions pretty well, until they inevitably spilled over.

He pulled her wooden chair between his legs, bringing her closer to his face. "Are you going to tell me why your ribs are bruised? I mean, shit... It's the same side that maniac cracked in college—"

Remy cut him off with her lips. After she had spent eight hours on a crappy two-engine plane, another three on a commercial flight then a million more in customs, she didn't have the energy for the unavoidable fight. She almost never did with Knox, because the man always played to win.

He growled and captured her lips between his.

"Oh goody, we're making out in public. Yeah for me," Doris fake cheered. Bogged down with an arm full of magazines and files, she fought her way into a chair at their table. Remy hadn't heard her come into the restaurant. "A Tom Collins, a White Russian and a shot of tequila," she snapped at the waitress across the empty room. "Did you two want anything?" Similar to a crazed squirrel, Doris swiveled her silver-covered head back and forth between them. "No? No...good."

Knox opened his eyes wide at Remy before turning away to hide his grin behind his hand.

"She's gorgeous," Doris barked at Knox.

"Gee, thanks, Dor, but I'm right here. And believe me when I say I love compliments," Remy said.

"Trust me, hon. That wasn't one. I'm equipped to deal with cokeheads, prostitutes and politicians, but not sports heroes cheating on perfect wives. That's why I try not to take on a certain type of client, as a general rule."

"Damn, girl, I'm going to be hard pressed not to like you," Remy retorted.

Knox cleared his throat, probably in an attempt to stop her from messing with the publicist. He knew better than anyone that poking the bear was her favorite drug.

Doris threw down the first magazine from the pack. "You take epic pictures of the world's worst crises then match them with dazzling words to make even my jaded ass care." She continued to throw magazine after magazine of Remy's work on the table. "Girls' education in Pakistan, abortion rights in Ireland, freaking Brexit," she listed. "I would be surprised if you didn't get nominated for a Pulitzer."

"Okay, that did it, dammit. Bring it in for a hug." Remy stood, but the sharp bolt of pain caused her to hunch over and grab her side.

Knox reached out to steady her.

"What's wrong?" The pinched expression on the woman's face quickly turned into anger. "What the hell did he do to you?" Doris slapped at him.

"No, no, it's okay." Remy caught the woman's hand in hers and held it. "Foreign airport. Heartbreaker here had nothing to do with it. I haven't seen him for a few weeks now."

"A month," he fake-coughed into his hand.

Ignoring Knox, Remy asked, "You good?" before she let the woman go.

Doris nodded. "It's just a trigger is all." She sat back down without offering anyone an apology.

"We all have them. It's cool," Remy assured her.

"Yeah, that's true. We do," Doris agreed.

While nodding at Doris, Remy gently rubbed Knox's leg. The energy, which had quickly morphed toward hostile, settled into a tepid awkward. They sat quietly until the waitress brought the fixer's drink order.

"Do you mind?" Remy reached for the White Russian. "Let's toast to escaping this mess with fewer scars than we came in with."

Doris picked up her Tom Collins. "To fewer scars." They touched glasses. Under the gaze of Knox's stink-eye, Remy chugged her drink. The doctor had prescribed her pain medication that she had no intention of taking. Of course, he didn't know that.

"Better?" Remy asked.

"Much." Doris straightened the wireless frame of her glasses that had slipped down her tiny nose and grabbed another magazine. Instead of *Time*, *National Geographic* or *The New Yorker*, she flung down a *People*, with Knox and a pop star on the cover. Then she chucked an *Us* magazine with the quarterback and a B-movie actress on top of it. "You cheated on the prom queen with low IQ trash."

"Oh, Doris" — Remy laughed — "harsh."

"Trust me. I know these girls. They're pretty stupid," the publicist admitted.

Knox shifted in his chair.

"I'll take your word for it." Remy smirked.

A twitch of a smile tugged at Doris' mouth. "Needless to say, it looks like ball boy over here needed a green card, and that's a big no-no to the average American."

"He didn't need one. I did."

"What?"

"Ball boy was doing me a solid, not the other way around. I needed Canadian citizenship because—"

"No, no, no." Doris freaked out again. "Never answer a question I didn't ask."

Remy glanced at Knox, who turned out to be absolutely no help. He shook his head and gazed out of the café window. "So…what do we do? Charades? 'Cause I got to tell you, Dor. I suck at that game."

Knox chuckled. To avoid joining him, Remy kept her eyes trained on the publicist.

"No, I just need plausible deniability. I'm also a lawyer."

"Why does *that* matter?" She felt lost. Jetlag definitely didn't help her current state of mind, but the conversation seemed to have taken a strange turn that she couldn't get a handle on.

"Yeah, I hear that a lot. Look, you two… Whatever the hell this is"—she gestured between them—"you need to go public in a big way. Get on those covers acting like you hit a rough patch and you're trying to work it out…" She paused to scratch her little bunny nose with the back of her hand. "Or fight like psychos and end it sooner rather than later."

"Wait a minute," Remy said. "You don't know why we got married, so—"

"Nuh-uh." Doris drank the rest of her Tom Collins then moved on to her shot. Throwing back her head, she made quick work of the tequila. "No questions means no replies." She pounded on her chest until she belched. "Excuse me. Once you two figure out what direction you want to take, let me know. In the meantime, I've got to scoot." She laid her business card on the table. "Hopefully this little issue doesn't get any bigger."

* * * *

After the hideous meeting with the publicist, they stepped into the brutal, snow-covered streets. The city plows had barely made a dent in the hard, dirty mess that had painted the whole city gray. Knox reached over to straighten the collar on the coat he had let her borrow. It swallowed her five-foot-nine frame, but she didn't have anything sturdy to wear. "Ready to hit the bed?"

"Don't you have that pub opening?" she asked.

His gaze darted down and to the right, avoiding her stare. "Yeah, it's no biggie. I'll send some celebratory cigars."

"We can still make it," she said.

"Rem." His face morphed into that judgmental, disappointed mask she hated. "You just got here."

"No problem. I need some new clothes then I'm good."

"Why do you need clothes?" Knox squinted his eyes.

"Because I don't have any." Since they'd been in such a rush to get to the clinic, he probably hadn't thought anything of her sporting his T-shirt and a pair of leggings she had dug out of her purse.

Without another word, he grabbed her hand and took her across the street to some trendy boutique.

Before they pushed open the door, they could hear the salesgirl's screams. "Holy shit, it's Gavin Knox!" The store associate danced from foot to foot with unbridled energy.

"Hi." He tossed her his supastar smile. "We just need a couple of things. Do you mind setting up a room for us?"

"Uh...uh m-my pleasure." She took off toward the back of the store at an impressive clip. Amused by the reaction Knox managed to get out of people, Remy reached for a ribbed black dress on the rack. He blocked her with his amazing body, and she rolled her eyes. Similar to a dog with a bone, Knox wouldn't let go.

"Credit cards?" he pushed.

"You know the answer to that." Every so often, Remy had to cancel out her cards and resort to using cash to avoid anyone tracking her. She attempted to dodge Knox's big body and reached around him. Considering that he moved fast for a living, he easily snaked her hand into his. *Dammit, that dress has my name on it.*

"Activity in your accounts came to an abrupt halt a few weeks ago."

"Just being cautious," she lied.

"It freaked me out." He stared at her, probably waiting for a confession.

"Your room's ready," the sales associate interrupted them.

Knox slid Remy a dirty look before he turned toward the girl. "Great! What's your name?" he asked with his best playboy smile.

"Kim." She giggled.

"Could you show my wife where to go then come back to help me pick out some stuff?"

"Sure…" The chick bobbed her head up and down in her best imitation of a sports figurine.

"Knox…" Remy sighed.

"I'm faster—and you hate doing this anyway." He smirked, which meant he had an idea of what he wanted to see her in.

"This way." Kim damn near snatched Remy's arm off. Reluctantly, she trailed behind the salesgirl, who unceremoniously dumped her at the door. "There's wine on ice," she called over her shoulder, practically tripping over her own feet to get back to Knox.

Remy slipped off his coat and took a seat on the chaise longue in the changing room. A sparkly chandelier hung above the white, plush, girly furniture, causing the room to resemble a rich woman's closet. Once she rolled Knox's coat into a ball and placed it under her head, her whole body relaxed. Weeks on the run from one place to another had finally caught up with her.

"Hey," he said. Surprised that she'd fallen asleep so fast, Remy sat straight up. "Let's go home," he said.

"Are you kidding?" Remy stretched with a yawn. "Best nap ever." She offered him a wan smile.

"Here." Knox held out a tank for her.

When she grabbed it, he didn't budge from his spot. "Are you seriously staying here?"

"What? Are you shy?" he inquired with a slightly mocking tone, raising his eyebrow. "You kicked me out of the doctor's office and you won't tell me what happened, so-o-o…"

Judging by his hardened glare, she figured she truly had no choice. Knox waited patiently for her to take off her shirt. Too tired for this crap, she pulled it over her head.

"Fuck, Remy," he whispered.

Ugly bruises colored her body. The doctor had given her a patch for her ribs to cover the small gash. "Your uncle?" he grumbled.

"Maybe the credit card tracking, but the rest is courtesy of the Rio police."

He ran his fingers along the side of her nasty, blueish-purple-colored bruise. It spread across the right flank of her body. "An underground rebellion had planned a protest for the assassination of an activist, Marielle Franco. The police, who were crazy corrupt, had gotten wind of it and had raided the favelas."

While he continued to study her, she stepped out of her pants, but thankfully the bruises on her legs weren't that bad. "Cops were crawling all over public transportation, which made it harder to get out of the city. They didn't want any reporters writing about it."

"What happened to Plan B? That's what you told me, that there's always a back-up, right? Or was that also a lie?" Knox's gaze glided up her body before his accusatory glare landed on her face. "All this time overseas, and you're honestly no safer over there than you are with me, here in the States?"

Remy softly caressed the side of his face. She hid so much from him. It seemed too hypocritical of her to jump out of the frying pan straight into the fire. "Someone sent out this mysterious bat signal, and my pick-up wasn't ready."

"So this is *my* fault?" He frowned. "If I hadn't texted you—"

"It's nobody's fault, Supastar. I'm cool." She stepped into the distressed jeans he had brought her and grabbed the tank she'd laid to the side. Holding in a groan, she slipped it over her head. She had been a little off her fleeing game, so the cops had caught up with her group at the trolley. Remy's ribs and back had gotten the brunt of it.

"How are you two doing in there?" Kim's chipper little voice called through the door.

Knox gritted his teeth and yanked it open. "Great," he said, with oodles of charm.

As he quickly transformed into a better mood for his favorite fan, Remy dug into her purse. She palmed a bottle of hair oil and squirted a few drops into her hand.

"There's a gold necklace in the case, three strands with circles at the bottom. Could you grab that for me?" Knox asked.

"My pleasure," Kim cooed.

Remy rubbed the oil through her curls and wound her huge mane into a top knot, securing it with a couple of rubber bands that she had on her wrist. Grabbing her gloss and eyeliner out of the magical sorting hat that she called a purse, she made her way to the mirror.

"If I'd known you were getting your ass kicked on a daily basis, there's no way I would have—" Knox began.

"What?" Her chest constricted. She hated to go back and forth with him about this crap. "We both know that the alternative is much worse."

He punched the air with a growl. "Screw this. Let's just go home. The guys will understand."

"No. You heard Doris." She slid the slick, pinkish-tone gloss across her lips and locked eyes with her superstar husband in the mirror. "We've got to figure out if we want to stay married or not."

Chapter Three

Annoyed by the music's hard bass, Knox ordered a drink at the grand opening of his fullback's sports bar, Murphy's Pub. Today had produced worse hits for him than his entire football career put together, which said a lot, considering he had taken some real blows on the field. He felt beat up.

First, the publicist had thrown him off with those stupid magazines. Then Remy's response had sealed the deal. She hadn't batted an eye at those pictures of him with other women, which meant he had played everything wrong.

What if she has already met someone else? The possibility of her with some other guy shredded his insides.

Truthfully, they had only gotten married to keep her alive. They needed to stay together long enough to get her a green card — or at least that was the way he had sold it to her. Knox took a hard swig of Patrón from his glass. Done with that drink in record time, he set it down in front of him and ordered another.

Beautiful and laid back, the girl of his dreams had offered him an easy out. Knox, on the other hand, had figured he would convince her to stick around. If that hadn't worked, he would simply knock her up with a few of his babies. Nevertheless, Remy had taken off to destinations unknown, foiling any of his attempts at a plan.

Knox had used every free minute of his time to track down his beautiful wife. Eventually, they had turned it into a game. No matter how remote the country, Knox had always found himself chasing Remy.

Throughout the football season, she had left clues to each destination, except for winter break. He had wanted to surprise her. Instead, he'd received the surprise. A simple vacation in Greece had opened his eyes to what Remy really did for a living. He believed the term was 'death chaser', but he couldn't be sure, since no one had ever explained it to him.

"Hey, man, I didn't think you'd make it," Jake cried, clearly drunk off his ass. "That press conference was a disaster." The team's favorite fullback waved a couple of his teammates over. After the big win, they'd had to attend the city parade, which had left the guys with no time to pump him for info. "What the hell was that old hack Artie getting at?"

Not quite loose enough to have this conversation, Knox hoped for a few more drinks. Honestly, he'd wanted to drown his anger the minute he had laid eyes on Remy's battered body. "Art used to be a real asshole when I first joined the team," he explained. "So I got his car towed a couple of times from the stadium. He's had it hard for me ever since."

"Maybe he has dementia or something, because I've never seen you with…well, anybody."

As more players wandered over, the beefy fullback laughed hard at his own joke. "Dre!" he called out. "Hard Knox is going to sue Artie's rinky-dink paper."

All the Mavericks gathered around the bar fairly quickly, with their wives and girlfriends in tow.

"Saying you need a green card..." Doug, one of the guards, said, loud and drunk. "I mean, when do Canadians need green cards?"

"Since forevah," the rookie Mooch muttered.

Knox chuckled and raised his hand to the bartender.

"Where's my girl?" Doug asked about his fiancée, who he never let out of his sight for more than five minutes.

"She's over there talking to some groupie nerd," Alli, Juan, the replacement QB's wife, answered. She was bossy to a bitter degree, and no one cared for her very much.

"Hey, Lisa, come here," Doug hollered. She stood near the door next to Remy. The raven-haired woman grabbed Remy's arm to pull her along.

The high heels, jeans and a sexy leather jacket he'd chosen for her complemented Remy's banging body and heartbreaker face. *If only I could keep her*, Knox groused in his head before he chugged back another drink. Ever since college, she'd continued to slip further and further away.

"Guys, you won't believe who this is," Lisa said.

"Be quiet," Doug snapped. "Hard Knox is talking about suing that paper for lying. What's that called?"

"Defamation, idiot."

"What did you say, rookie?" Doug's badger face scrunched into an ugly red mask of anger.

Jake put his hand on the roided-out freak's chest. "Chill out," he told him. "No one's fighting in my bar. Sorry, Knox. Go ahead."

"The article got it half right."

"Crap! You don't have a green card? The government is going to deport you. Dammit," Jake hissed. "That damn wall…"

"Not that part." Knox tipped his glass to her. "Everyone, Hot Wife. Hot Wife, everyone."

"Hi." She waved at the bar with a twinkle in her brilliant brown eyes. "Code name Remy."

"Shoot," someone said behind him, "I was going to hit on her."

"Yeah, me too," a different voice responded. Not entirely sure if that one was a dude, Knox turned around but didn't find the offender.

"Uh, I thought I heard you mention being a writer or something?" the relief QB's wife asked.

"Kind of, sort of," Remy replied, with a deliriously bright smile.

"Anything good? I mean, we've never seen you before now," the bossy blonde continued to fire off questions in that nasally baby tone that he hated.

"Yeah, that's what I was trying to tell you." Lisa's enthusiasm bubbled over. "She was featured in one of my classes."

"Oh, you're a student?" Remy asked her. "Which school?"

"No," Doug grunted, before he yanked his fiancée toward him. "This one gets bored and goes up to Chicago State, but she's not enrolled anywhere. She thinks it's cute." The enthusiasm on Lisa's face evaporated, which made Knox hate the douchebag even more.

"Cool!" Remy cheered. "I should have done that."

"Why the hell would that be cool?" bossy Alli snorted. "What's the point?"

"Steve Jobs did it. I mean, why pay if you don't have to?" Remy shrugged.

Lisa bit her lip, but Knox could still make out the smile she tried to hide. She probably didn't want to get too amped, because the wives had a hierarchy that Remy had trampled all over. Normally, no one ever put the blonde in her place—at least, no one in this group. The other half of the wives who wouldn't tolerate that crap generally didn't hang out with them.

"Well, my class... I mean the class mentioned an exhibit. The Art Institute is displaying work from photojournalists around the world, and you're featured," Knox told her.

"Exsqueeze me?" Remy looked straight at him.

"Zing," he responded from his favorite movie, *Wayne's World*, with a laugh, finally feeling the effects of the Patrón. "I was going to surprise you, but—" He stopped himself from mentioning that she hadn't called him in weeks.

After the playoffs, he had planned to hire a guide and track her down. Thankfully, old man Artie had solved the mystery of his lost wife. He should buy the old buzzard a steak dinner for delivering her straight to his doorstep...or shove his foot up the reporter's ass. Either scenario worked for him.

"That still doesn't explain why we haven't heard anything about you until now," the blonde whined.

Officially over the whole Q-and-A mess, Knox reached into the sea of giants to grab her. "We've got to get going. Remy has jetlag." Moving the mass of players with the force of his body, he led her out of the door. "Great opening, man. We'll catch you later."

"What about Barbados? Are you still coming?"

Knox opened his mouth to respond.

"We don't have room for a plus one on the plane," Alli cut him off.

"I'm sure if—" His relief quarterback tried to stop his wife, but the blonde bowled him over.

"The promoters made limited arrangements for our accommodations, and since I set this whole thing up, I should know. Besides, all the starters made a commitment, so... Sorry... What was your name again, sweetie?" she asked sarcastically.

"Remy," Allison's husband hissed.

"But I don't remember," Alli muttered, loud enough for everyone to hear.

"And on that note," Knox said, throwing up the peace sign and ushering Remy to the door, "we'll catch you guys later."

Night had fallen upon the city at an unbelievably fast rate. Winter barely held a good eight hours of sunlight in the day. Knox figured they could catch a cab back home.

"Nice meeting you, Remy." Mooch exited the building with them.

"Hey, wait up." Knox jogged toward the kid's SUV. Thanks to the tequila, it took a minute for his brain to manufacture a good idea.

Chapter Four

Ambient lighting illuminated the wall-sized photograph of Remy's work in the Chicago Art Institute.

"Wow," Mooch said.

The three of them stood in front of a large-scale picture. Girls in uniforms were running from religious radicals. It showed one child, who had fallen, while another tried to help her up. In the background, a young teacher was ushering them into the school. "What happened? I mean, after?" Knox asked.

"They made it inside safely."

"And you?" He grabbed Remy's hand, intertwining their fingers while they moved on to the next picture.

"*Goat Herder*," Mooch read off the card underneath the shot. The front of the picture showed an old man herding his goats across a road. Hundreds of refugees waited patiently for them to pass.

"Do I need to ask?"

"They made it and I made it," Remy told him.

"Amazing!" Mooch said to the last one.

Pure blue skies highlighted ten black nuns dressed in all-white habits. An ancient-looking woman held a dead child wrapped in a shroud and the sign of the cross appeared on the cloth from the sunlight. It was stunning.

"*Ghana*," Knox read off the card. "You were in *Africa*?"

"Passing through," she muttered.

The museum had closed two hours earlier but Knox had managed to call in a favor and got them to open Remy's exhibit. Of course, scoring championships for the city didn't hurt his ability to get them into hard places. Finished with their walk-through, Knox thanked the guard, who opened the door for them to leave.

"What's this about Barbados?" she asked.

"Some liquor company is sponsoring an all-expenses paid trip to the island for promotions," Knox told her.

"Are we going?" Remy asked with a hopeful tone.

"Stop me if I'm wrong, but didn't you just land less than twelve hours ago?"

Completely ignoring him, she turned toward Mooch. "What about you?"

"Uh" — he ducked his head — "I've got a lot on my plate right now."

"But you won. You should come with," she pushed.

Knox knew what the kid meant. He had a ton of legal bills and court dates to deal with. It was something to do with an abusive, alcoholic stepfather or some such crap. Knox didn't have all of the details, but he knew Mooch didn't have the cash to pay for everything. Unfortunately, he hadn't exactly gotten the best contract.

"I doubt they would want me to crash. It's just for the star players—"

Knox shook his head, cutting him off. "There's no point fighting this. What Remy wants, Remy gets. I'll have someone call you with the details."

Mooch hid his smile and laughed behind his hand. "If you're sure, man, thanks." Knox bumped knuckles with the kid. "Do you need a ride home?"

"No, we're cool," Knox told him. "I ordered an Uber." The cold air seemed to chill his bones. He guided Remy toward the waiting car and kissed her on the head. "Stay out of it, baby."

"What?" she answered, a little too sweetly for his taste.

"Doug's a douche. Believe me… We all know it, but Lisa's *his* fiancée and that's it. Whatever crazy vibe you picked up on—"

"So you felt it, too, with Mooch?" Her diminutive laugh turned into a hard belly shaker that ended up in hiccups.

"Argh-h-h." Knox dropped his head back with a groan.

* * * *

Winter had a strong hold on the city.

Puffy clouds separated Knox's view from downtown, as a couple of stars sparkled through the foggy blanket above his condo. Soft tones of blue mixed with dark wood made up the color scheme of his place. The whole design seamlessly blended the gorgeous view of the city into his home. Nervous energy coursed through his veins, which made it hard for him to sleep, so he'd decided to stop trying. Knox sat at his dining room table to FaceTime his parents. As they'd been night owls since he was young, he had no doubt his parents would still be up.

A distinguished version of himself picked up the phone. "My boy," William Knox said with a slight French accent.

"Papa."

"How do you like Doris?" Dad smiled.

"Uh-h." Knox rubbed his hand through his wet hair. The cool shower had done nothing to fix his relentless hard-on. "She's different."

"Highly recommended. Did she give you good advice?"

"Good is going a bit far," Knox told him.

"Is that Gavin?" His mom asked off screen.

"Yes, he's complaining about the publicist I sent him." Dad turned away from the camera.

"I didn't complain, per se."

"How is our girl? Is she there?" Claire Knox grabbed the tablet out of her husband's hands, leaving Knox with a shot of the floor and ceiling before her lovely face appeared.

"Asleep." He smiled, not in the least happy about the circumstances but thrilled she was near.

"Have you seen her latest?"

If she meant Remy's bruised and battered body, then yes. "No, I've been a little busy." He decided to avoid bitching about her choice of professions, because he had enough crap on his plate.

"As soon as you get a chance… It's epic."

"Yes, Mama."

"Tell her to call me." Knox found that request odd, but he didn't comment on it. "Kiss to you, kiss to Remy."

Once she'd handed the tablet back, his kind father switched to a disciplinary frown. "Now why are you calling me so late, ruining my Netflix and chill time?"

"Too much," he groaned at the thought of it before he got down to brass tacks with the old man. "We need a charter to Barbados in the morning."

"Is this the fixer's idea?" Dad's asked, pushing his glasses high onto his head.

"No, it's a team thing that Remy wants to go on."

"Ah, of course! There's a festival. It's a perfect idea for a piece. Anything else?"

Annoyed that his dad had understood his wife's motives quicker than he ever could, Knox rubbed his face in frustration. "Can you find out who leaked our marriage certificate to that hack Artie?"

"Oh." Dad adjusted his position, causing him to go out of frame. "We can only guess." His face froze before he came back into focus and he seemed evasive.

"But her uncle?" Knox cleared his throat that suddenly felt sandpaper dry.

"It's time."

Frustrated that no one wanted to give him straight answers, he tapped his fingers against the oak table. "If I recall correctly, even you agreed that the only way to keep her safe was to keep her out of the States."

"Back then, yes. Now? No. Either you want her to be brilliant for the world or brilliant for you. Besides, I'm looking for you to give me a couple of sweet grandchildren."

Knox tried to laugh off the needles of tension that rose inside of him. "Greg has given you two, old man. You're fine," he stated, bringing up his brother's super-active kids.

With a twinkle in his eyes, his father glanced around before he put his mouth to the screen. "The operative word is 'sweet'. Now go to sleep."

The screen went black. William Knox, the prime minister of Canada, had hung up on him.

Chapter Five

True to his word, Knox had arranged for a private charter to take them to Barbados. Barely a whole day after she'd arrived in Chicago, Remy found herself boarding another flight. A couple of Knox's team members had joined them on the ride to the island, leaving everyone else to travel with Alli, as had been originally planned.

For the most part, everything had gone off without a hitch, at least until they'd landed. After the seven-hour flight, the small group had fully expected to freshen up and join the rest of the team. However, Alli had other plans. None too pleased with the travel defectors, the football wife had cancelled everyone's room who hadn't traveled with the original group.

As sticky heat clung to her skin, Remy tried to ignore the tense energy swirling all around them. Surprised that they were still invited to dinner, the team sat awkwardly at a huge table in the garden of a rum distillery.

"Explain to me again how our reservations got mysteriously canceled," Lashonda, wife to Andre, the running back, demanded. Remy had liked the sexy Amazon on sight.

"Well, when you missed the plane," Alli wagged her finger at them, as if they were naughty children, "I assumed you were no longer coming."

"Forgive me for being obtuse, but where the hell are we?" Lashonda asked. Andre silently reached over and removed the silverware from in front of his wife.

"A rum distillery. If you had flown with us, you would have caught the tour," Alli sang.

Remy locked eyes with Knox across the table. His blue eyes bored into hers over the rim of his third glass of liquor. He'd been distant on the plane and had seemed even more remote since they'd arrived. He only broke eye contact when the notification on his phone went off.

"So, where the hell are we supposed to sleep? The beach?" one of the other wives jumped in.

Within a short amount of time, Remy had figured out that the men did their best to stay out of the women's disagreements. Not one player had gotten involved. Apparently, the women were split into two groups—the working moms and the housewives.

"I know I'm not about to pass out sitting here in the middle of a rain forest with a sweater on," another wife complained. "I promise I'll get naked first."

Biting into a breadstick, Remy prayed to be out of the way of whoever threw the first punch.

"Hey!" Knox addressed the whole table. "Everyone who flew with us is now booked into the hotel. You can check in with my name at the front desk."

A cheer went up at his announcement.

"But the Wave Festival? I thought they... Never mind." Leaning back in her seat, Alli pouted.

As Knox pushed back from the table, he nodded toward the pathway leading to the gardens. "We're going to check out, I don't know... What is that? A waterfall? If the food comes, go ahead and start without us." Pretty sure they wouldn't be back in enough time, Remy quickly chugged down the rest of her rum.

"What did you say this place was again?" Lashonda asked.

"We've been over this a hundred times. It's a distillery," Alli repeated.

"Nobody's stupid, Allison. This place is a fucking plantation," Remy said. Unable to stifle it any longer, a fit of giggles attacked her sleep-wearied soul. "Sorry," she apologized to the group. "It's the heat." Knox joined her at the end of the table.

"No, it's not," Lashonda hissed. "You know this bitch has us sitting at a plantation like the shit is cute."

"What's the problem? Irish slaves worked in the fields as well." Alli waved her hand dismissively.

"Oh God," one of the men croaked.

Remy held the side of her bruised ribs, nearly toppling over. "Stop," Knox whispered a chuckle into her ear. "You'll only make it worse." He wrapped his arm around her waist and pulled her along.

"My ribs or the situation?" She snorted.

"Both," he told her.

After they'd made it to the path, she finally petered out. "Are they always like this?"

"Not sure. I don't do the socializing thing too often."

Remy sobered once she realized that Knox probably avoided group events due to her absence.

Tiki torches lined the path to a cove and colorful lights illuminated the cascading water. Knox grabbed her hand and pulled her toward the thunderous sounds of the running rapids. "I saw this on the map near the entrance."

He guided her to the out-of-the-way spot, where the falling water sprinkled against her skin. Before they had left the table, Remy had fully understood what he wanted. "What if there are cameras?"

He kissed her, cutting off her words and traced the bottom of her lip with his tongue. Flying on adrenaline for the past two days, Remy craved his touch. "I scoped out the angles when we came in," he panted. "Two outside, not inside. Come on, baby. I promise the romantic shit later, but I'm about to explode." Slipping his tongue into her mouth, he fumbled with the hardware on her jeans. "Blue balls and their incessant bitching do not mix," he muttered between his frantically undressing her.

Light-headed from need, Remy tried to speak, but Knox's demanding touch overrode her senses.

"Railing," he rambled. "Hold on to it. I'll try not to slam into your pussy too hard." He rubbed her clit from outside her jeans. The warm sensation from his thumb made her buck against his touch.

While he roamed his hands all over her body, he sucked on her neck. She slapped away the part of her senses that cried for a modicum of decency. Horny as hell, she popped the button on her pants and pushed the denim material down past the hump of her ass.

Knox blew out a ragged breath.

Before he placed his hand back between her legs, he yanked her bra down and rolled her nipple between his fingers. How he got his hand under her tank that fast she'd never know.

"Hold onto the rail." He fumbled with his belt buckle. "So fucking wet." In a slow and deliberate rhythm, he tapped her clit with his index finger.

Manipulating her pussy, he slipped his finger into her slit. Pulling in and out, he brought her near the brink before he took his cock and slammed it inside her.

"Fuck!" No drug-induced high could ever touch the way his thick rod filled her.

"Whose pussy is this?"

From the minute the publicist had set those magazines in front of them, she'd known where this would go. No matter how hard Knox tried to twist his guilt into jealousy, she wouldn't allow him to interfere with her orgasm. "Whose pussy is this?" he demanded.

Ignoring the pain in her muscles from her bruised body, she pushed back against him.

As Knox wrapped his forearm around her, he pounded her from behind. Unable to hold herself up, she allowed the clawing waves of pleasure to overwhelm her. Little by little, her world came back into focus.

"Don't come in me," she mumbled.

He increased his speed. Groaning heavy against her ear, Knox loaded her pussy with his seed before he stilled inside her body.

Remy attempted to stamp down the anger that had begged to come out since yesterday. Knox knew the rules. Without words, she pulled her jeans back up. When he reached out to help straighten her tank top, she slapped his hand away.

"I'm sure you're still on birth control." He chuckled. "If not, then yay for me. Hey!" She ducked past the waterfalls and hit the path that led to the taxi stand. "Come on, Remy. I'm hungry."

"Then go eat." A glob of stickiness pooled in the crotch of her jeans. It grossed her out.

Super-fast, the athlete had a hold of her arm. "We came together, so we stay together," he growled. "I know you're used to that shit, but humor the stupid jock you married."

Snatching her arm from his grip, she stomped down the trail. Remy knew Knox was itching for a fight to assuage his guilt, but she refused to hand it to him.

"Not real sure, but I'm pretty positive cum-stained jeans aren't the proper dinner attire."

"Why not?"

"What are you doing, marking me like a dog? I'm not wearing any underwear," Remy grunted.

"Maybe you should stop hanging out in places where you have to leave your panties behind." As his sweet, baby blue eyes flashed an ominous shade of navy, he shoved his face close to hers.

"Oh, I forgot… That's what we're doing, changing the narrative of your fuck up." She dramatically sighed at the psych one-o-one crap that he was attempting to pull on her. "Okay, Knox, I'm the villain and you're perfect again…" Remy imitated a magician. "Abra-fucking-cadabra."

It must have taken a minute for the alcohol to fully kick into the giant's system. Usually, Knox didn't show any of the telltale signs right away. Remy turned toward the distillery's entrance, hoping to catch a cab without him.

* * * *

Carrots… His wife hated those pretty passionately. Knox could count on his fingers the things that Remy hated. Not big on clearing the air, she would gloss over small problems until they became mountains. However, nutting in her body with no way for her to clean up probably rated number one on her 'reasons for being pissed off' list. It might have been childish, but he didn't care.

By the time he'd arrived at the hotel and grabbed the keycard from the front desk, her energy practically slapped at him from across the lobby. He trailed her from a distance into the elevator and up to their room.

She stepped to the side to allow him to open the door. Unwilling to play her passive-aggressive game any longer, he pulled her in front of him and locked her in with his arms. "What's the rush?" Knox knew every part of her, every inch of her, and he believed without a shadow of a doubt that he needed to let her cool down. Unfortunately, the DNA coding that wrote the script for his stubborn streak wouldn't allow him to stop.

"Open the door, Knox."

"You didn't answer my question." Remy tried to use her forehead to push him back. He snorted at her adorable, kitten-like attempt to move him.

"It's sticky between my legs. The shit's disgusting. Open the door!"

Undeterred by her temper tantrum, he fixed his gaze on her heart-shaped face and waited for her to reply.

"How about this… Once you sober up, we'll have that knock-down, drag-out fight you want so bad." She snatched the keycard out of his hand and shoved it into the slot. "Until then, screw you, Knox." Opening the door, she slipped into their suite, slamming it shut behind her.

Wildly underestimating that play, he dropped his head against the wood and groaned. "Remy!" he shouted. They had been able to score only one card because the hotel's machine had shorted out. She possessed the lone key to their room. "Seriously, open the door!"

"Hey, Knox!" his linebacker shouted down the hall. "We're getting a poker game together in the bar. You want in?"

Since spending the rest of his night in the hallway wasn't an option, he figured it couldn't hurt. "Sure." Pushing away from the closed door, he headed to the elevator bay. At a record-breaking two hours and thirty minutes, Knox had already tired of the scenic lull of paradise.

Chapter Six

Remy slipped out of the shower and snagged one of the linen robes off the back of the door. Purposely knocking the spare one onto the tiles, she stepped on it. No matter how hard he banged on the door, she had no intention of letting Knox into the room.

Tropical heat from the balcony blew into the suite. Semi-comfortable with the temperature, Remy didn't mind the humidity. Knox, on the other hand, would hate it. Turning on the air conditioner to cool down their suite was an option, but at the moment, she simply didn't care. Maybe he was right about her passive-aggressive tendencies. They were something she promised to explore in depth about herself one day, but not today—and probably no time soon.

"Come on, girl. Open up! We look like hookers out here."

After pulling the belt tight on the robe, she opened the door to a crowded hallway of football wives. "To what do I owe the pleasure?" Remy smirked at the half-dressed squad of women. While three of them had on cute matching pajamas, the rest sported the same complimentary hotel robe that she wore.

"We want somewhere to gossip, and you have a suite."

"Uh, I thought Knox got suites for everyone who flew with us on the plane?" She leaned against the door frame, already amused by their unexpected appearance. On one hand, she could sit and be pissed at Knox all night or she could be entertained with nonsense. *A no brainer*, Remy figured.

"Yeah, we want to do it without Allison, and since she clearly despises you, we figured your room was safe." Lashonda barged her way in. "And Knox is playing poker with the guys, so-o-o-o..."

"We brought wine," a guard's wife called from the back of the crowded hallway. For such a tiny thing, Remy wondered how she made the height difference work with her husband.

"Why not?" She let the rest of them pile into the room. "I can use a drink."

* * * *

Although Remy was slightly tipsy but totally amused after her second glass of merlot, the football wives showed her no signs that they were slowing down. Since she often traveled alone, she rarely indulged. She had become a pro at nursing the same drink for hours.

Between the wine and the vodka, Lashonda had braided Remy's hair. Sensing that she was already half in the bag, Remy reconsidered the woman's overly generous offer. "Ladies," she began, "I don't know what the itinerary is for this weekend, but—"

"That's easy. Allison is going to hold us hostage until we all agree to do this reality show she's pushing," the one who had 'hot librarian' written all over her replied.

"None of our husbands are on board, and now that you've showed up—" Lashonda finished.

"Wait a minute! What do *I* have to do with this?"

"Knox is the quarterback," her honorary hair stylist explained.

"Ow!" Remy flinched at the sudden pain.

"Sorry, girl. How the hell are you tender-headed with all of this hair?"

"Because I don't yank it out by the root," she muttered.

"My touch is very tender, I'll have you know."

Remy glared over her shoulder and wondered once again if she'd underestimated Lashonda's level of drunkenness.

"Stop fidgeting and listen up," the football wife demanded. "Player stats and popularity are directly correlated with the hierarchy of the wives."

"How long you've been married means basically nothing if your husband's stats suck." The sexy librarian held her glass out for another drink before she shrugged and grabbed the whole bottle of tequila. "Which means that you're the number one wife… Even if he is cheating on you."

"Lacy!" the tiny one hissed.

"Not that I think he is! I mean, pictures don't mean anything. Also, if I were to judge by the way he eye-banged you across the table at dinner—"

"And probably *really* banged you in the rainforest," Lashonda added. Remy held her hand up for a high-five. The football wife landed the affirmative loud smack to the middle of her palm.

"Public sex," Remy gasped in mock horror. "And here I thought we were being discreet."

The women joined Remy in a laugh, until a big, ugly sob from the librarian silenced the group.

"We used to be like that, me and Roy," she cried, while sipping from the bottle of tequila. "But that bitch!"

"Oh hell," Lashonda muttered. "Not that Remy doesn't want to be filled in on The Carl's Junior girl, but we're trying to keep it light. Right, Lace?"

"Yeah," she sniffled. "Light and tight."

"Here's the dirty… Alli is going to either ice you out or cozy up to you, and considering how Knox hates the press more than anyone…"

"Iced," the wives screamed in unison. The little one even dragged her finger across her throat and made the death sign, with the lolling tongue.

"All done." Lashonda nudged her shoulder. Remy got up from the chair and went to the mirror above the couch. Fully prepared to lie, Remy smiled at her reflection. She absolutely loved the long twists.

"Good, huh? I do my best work drunk." The wife beamed.

"Ah-h-h," she murmured, speechless and amazed at how pretty the braids had turned out.

"Right? I was a hair stylist before I became a fashion stylist and got knocked up a whole bunch of times by a sex addict, so-o-o-o…" Lashonda leaned sidewise on the arm of the couch. "Sometimes I miss it." She sighed before she fell onto the cushions.

Still admiring her hair, Remy did a little dance. "This is perfect for the Wave Festival."

"You've got tickets?" the tiny one whined. "Great! You have all of the fun while we're here with our fingers up our butts listening to Alli pitch that stupid show."

"Actually, I have to work, but I scored extra tickets if you guys want to come."

"Yes, a thousand times yes," Lashonda said in a sing-songy tone. "Is it cool if we bring Lisa? She would be here, but—"

"Doug rarely lets her out of his sight." Librarian dabbed at her eyes.

"Why not?" Happy that the conversation had naturally turned toward the girl, she completely ignored Knox's advice to stay out of it. "I mean, what's the story with those two, anyway?"

Chapter Seven

As techno music blared across the muddy field, at least ninety degrees of tropical heat beamed down on them. Barely clothed bodies danced to a drug-induced beat. Eight out of eleven starters for the Mavericks, including Mooch, stood away from the dancers and tried to map out a food plan. Tired and grouchy, Knox felt the beginning signs of sunstroke in his not-so-distant future.

The team had stayed up late playing poker, reminiscing about their epic season. Even though Knox had won a ton of money, he'd still managed to sulk most of the night.

"We've been doing these promotional vacations for a while now and I've never seen our wives this happy."

"Shonda warned me that if this sucked, we were out," Andre said. "No more tours with the team." The wives danced in a tight circle in the middle of the clearing. *Everyone except Remy.* He scanned the crowd but didn't see her.

"Knox's wife has been around less than a week and scored us tickets to the biggest festival of the year," he heard one of the guys say.

"Yeah, well, no one really asked her to," Doug grumbled.

Knox squinted from the bright rays of the sun to stare at the ungrateful, bloated mess of a man. Stinky and swaying on his heels, his teammate appeared halfway out of his mind. None of them knew how he had passed their annual drug test.

"You didn't have to come," Knox responded.

"Who else would watch over Lisa?" Doug threw Mooch a shitty look before he went back to glaring at the wives in a psychotic manner. Officially done dealing with the hophead, he searched the crowd for his wife.

"She's over there." Mooch pointed to the DJ booth. Blending in seamlessly with the vibe of the crowd, she stood with her camera one level lower than the stage. Long braids flowed over her shoulder and down the back of her crop-top blouse. Finishing the ensemble off with her flowy skirt and sandals, she looked flawless.

"Hey, check out those horny toads," one of the guys remarked about a group of dudes who were inching closer to the circle of wives.

"I'll take care of it," Doug growled.

Andre caught him by the shoulder. "Slow your roll, Romeo." He laughed. "We'll just have to send in a blocker."

Knox slapped Mooch on the chest. "You're up."

"Oh, come on. That shit's embarrassing."

"Yeah, rookie," Andre called out, leading Doug toward the food vendors, "protect the prize."

Hanging his head in defeat, Mooch fought his way into the massive mob. Impressed by the kid's grace, Knox figured any one of their teammates would have resorted to mowing down the sea of gyrating partiers.

As the rookie worked his way into the chaos, Knox found his gaze wandering back to Remy. She kept her camera focused on the crowd. He had a pretty good idea what she was up to.

"Showtime." Jake tapped him on the shoulder. Mooch had arrived a few seconds after the little pervs had zeroed in on the group of wives. He picked off the boldest of the bunch fairly quickly. Ready to retaliate, the guy took in Mooch's size and obviously decided against that tussle.

With a serious face, Mooch threw his hands wide and danced hard. MC Hammering the circle, he went around the girls with an impressive beat, knocking off the encroaching group of men one by one.

The sight of the six-foot-four-inch cornerback's aggressive moves amused the crap out of all of them. Humping, thumping and bumping around the clueless idiots who had the bad luck to violate their women, Mooch put on such a show that Knox and his teammates laughed to the point where they were close to tears.

"Maybe we can get Remy to do the rest of these from now on." Jake choked and held his stomach, nearly doubled over with laughter.

"No shit. Alli sucks at it," one of the other players responded.

Drying up from the humor fairly quickly, Knox sought out Remy once again. Shielding her eyes from the sun, she was staring directly at their group. As his eyes locked with hers, he tried to figure out if something had changed.

Does she want to stay married or not?

* * * *

During the off season, the players allowed themselves a small amount of leeway in their diets, but nothing too extreme, since it hurt like hell to get back on track. He was positive that he had drunk his weight in alcohol, and a hard drumbeat kicked around in his head. To knock the edge off the incessant pain, Knox mixed himself a Bloody Mary.

As the numbers on the wall clock blurred, Remy stepped out of the bedroom. They'd had two more days in paradise and had spent less than a couple of hours in each other's presence.

"Nice, Knox. It's not even noon. At least you're getting a jump on the brunch crowd."

"Straight hair… Guess you won't be sweating away that blow-out!" He took a swig of the filthy concoction. Since he was already on shaky ground with her, he should have held his tongue, but he couldn't help it.

"Look at the Canadian knowing shit."

Pushing his sunglasses on top of his head, he felt his anger slowly swell. "You meant 'white boy' and you know it."

"I would have said it if I'd meant it." Remy's gaze never wavered from his. He drained his glass and took in the sight of her body-hugging sundress. Unable to distinguish what made him unhappy with her most at the moment, he decided that it must be everything. Remy's tab had stacked to an astronomical degree.

The wives had split into factions. Normally, the men veered clear of their petty arguments or infighting. Instead of allowing his wife to slip out of the range of blame, he added it to the list of grievances he had already compiled in his head.

Licking the hard liquor off his lips, he leaned across the suite's bar. "For the last time, sweetheart, whose pussy is this?"

Every muscle on her face drew taut. "Do you really want to go there?"

"Tell me. Have you been with somebody else? I want to know if I'm wasting my time."

"Says the man with the community dick."

Physically flinching from the sting of her words, he gritted his teeth. "You know I would never —"

"According to *US Weekly*, *People* magazine or even the world, for that matter, you did."

"It's just that I didn't know that it would go —"

"International?" She sneered. "Because football might not be a thing overseas, but tone-deaf pop stars are."

At the time, the whole publicity stunt had seemed like a good idea. Of course, his brilliant father had warned him against such nonsense. Knox shoved his hand through his hair and fought against his rapidly unraveling emotions. He'd had no clue their marriage certificate would get leaked.

"When those magazines hit the table, you didn't so much as blink at the covers," he told her.

"Okay, let's do this." She closed in the space between them. Mere inches away, he had no choice but to face her. "I started masturbating… I think it was freshman year in college." Remy put her hand to her chin and rolled her eyes upward, pretending as if she didn't remember. "Most teens start sooner, but after my parents died, my anxiety was off the charts. And I had that boyfriend in high school, so I didn't really need to do it that much then."

A flutter in his chest shortened his breath. If she confessed to cheating, he would lose it. "Remy," he growled, before he sucked in an inhuman amount of air.

Funny, in retrospect he'd believed he could handle that part. However, the mere thought of another man touching her drove him straight bonkers.

"After we got married, we had those long-ass football season droughts where you couldn't fly out to see me." Leaning casually against the bar, she flipped her hair. "Training camp, draft week, promotional tours…"

He tried to move around her to gain perspective, but she stepped in front of him.

"Okay," Knox said. His tightly controlled voice sounded foreign to his own ears, "I don't need to know. Just go do whatever you had planned. I'm going to bed."

"If I came back to the States, it would have been less time apart, but there's this maniac trying to kill me, and—"

"Remy!" he shouted. "If this shit in any way ends with you fucking someone else—"

"Vibrators are great!" she continued, without missing a beat. "But it's hard to find batteries in some of these countries. And the Internet for good porn? Forget about it."

"Holy shit! If you don't stop talking…" Pinching the bridge of his nose, he dropped his head back and counted way past ten.

"So, you'd think if I couldn't get dick or use a vibrator, that at the very least this asshole I married could do would be to pick up the phone, whether it was three a.m. or six p.m." — Remy's voice trembled — "no matter who he's sleeping next to."

As regret crept into his psyche and weighed on him, tears pooled in her big brown eyes and slipped down those supermodel-high cheekbones. He'd known better than to pull that manipulative crap in the first place, but months without her had played tricks on him. No better than the worst asshole on his team, he reached out to touch her. Remy quickly slipped out of his reach. Feeling useless, he shoved his hands into his jean pockets.

Knox knew he deserved this… He deserved worse.

"I picked up every time," he whispered, sounding lame, even to his own ears.

"That's the only reason we're not divorced…yet." She turned on her heel and left, slamming the door behind her.

Chapter Eight

Tears blurred the numbers on the panel. Remy swiped at her eyes and hit floor number five. Thankfully, no one had joined her in the cab, allowing her enough time to pull herself together.

Months ago, she had caught wind of those magazines with Knox on the cover and she'd immediately known his end goal.

He wanted her home.

She hadn't been back to America in years. Apparently, the long distance between them had taken its toll.

"Message received," she muttered. The doors to the elevator opened, and Remy stepped onto a floor she didn't recognize. Quiet storefronts lined this level, along with high-priced hotel suites. Since it was still fairly early, the rush of people probably wouldn't pick up until the afternoon.

"Hey, Remy." Mooch stepped out of the convenience store. He seemed almost as lost she did.

"Is the Internet café on this floor?" she asked.

"No, I think that's on seven, but don't quote me on it."

She needed to check her email but was still without a phone. Usually she would use Knox's. Needless to say, her current mood wouldn't allow her to even request simple directions to the bathroom from him.

"Thanks for the tickets to the festival. It was fun," Mooch said shyly. "This is my first vacation with the team, but I hear it's the best one they've had so far."

The elevator bell chimed. Offering him a tight smile, Remy backed into the cab.

"Hey," Mooch gently grabbed her arm, "that's going down."

She glanced over her shoulder at a man in a baseball cap. When he tilted his head up enough for her to see his face, she stumbled. As her heart skipped a beat, she scrambled to put distance between herself and the elevator bay.

"Are you okay?" Mooch asked.

Before the doors could fully close, Remy took off.

* * * *

Knox studied the bathroom mirror. Red-rimmed eyes and a five o'clock shadow three times over—heavily skating on a full-grown beard—stared back at him. He brushed his teeth, hoping that would help get rid of the grimy feel, but he had no such luck. His freshly clean mouth didn't help him. Knox still felt he placed first in the local creep competition for his poor behavior.

Someone pounded at the suite's door, interrupting the current bitch session inside his head. Maybe some sleep would work, but he doubted it. Although he was pretty sure Remy had her keycard, there didn't seem to be any way to escape the incessant banging.

Covering his face from the harsh island sun that penetrated the room, he stalked toward the door and flung it open. "What?"

"Is Remy here?" Mooch huffed out of breath.

"No, man, why?"

"We were at the elevators and she took off. I think she saw someone she knew or something. I don't know, but it was weird."

Doused with bone-chilling fear, he grabbed his shirt off the bar stool. "What did he look like?" Already out of their suite, Knox headed for the stairs.

"I'm not sure. I didn't get a real good look at him, but she seemed…I don't know, skittish." Mooch shrugged. "Scared, I mean. I wouldn't have come up here trying to find her, but—"

"But what?" Knox shouted.

"It kind of looked like he was trying to get out of the elevator to grab her. I don't know. I could be wrong."

"What floor?" He yanked the disgusting alcohol- and cigar-soiled shirt over his head.

"Five. She wanted the Internet café but got turned around."

"Do me a favor. Catch the elevator to that floor. I'll take the stairs. Let me in when you get there." Knox opened the door to the stairwell and took off. They were only six floors up from the fifth. The alcohol was probably slowing him down, but not by much. He took the steps two and three at a time.

As memories from that moment he had found her broken in the parking lot at his college apartment assailed him, Knox peered over the railing to the lower floors.

Mooch stood in the doorway.

"Head toward the casino," he barked at the rookie once he'd made it to that level. "I'll check out the suites over here."

A slow trickle of people were shopping on that floor, but the kid easily maneuvered around them. Knox rushed to the end of the corridor. A tight right took him to the suites overlooking the gardens.

Glancing back and forth, he found what he needed.

"Hi," he said to the maid. She smiled timidly but didn't say anything back. "Did you just start this room?"

"Yes."

"Where were you before this one?"

She pointed across the hall.

"Can you let me into that one for a quick second? I think I left my card."

Appearing hesitant to grant his request, Knox gave her his most sincere smile to convince her. "I'll be in and out, promise."

"Okay." She moved around her cleaning cart and scanned him into the room. Hoping to put her at ease, Knox attempted to keep the stupid grin on his face. He probably appeared nothing less than crazy.

"Remy," he whispered once he'd slipped into the room. "It's me, Remy."

Although similar to their suite, this one was slightly bigger, with a garden view. Knox stood in the outer sitting area and listened before he headed to the master.

"Remy," he called again. Knox peeked into the bathroom but saw nothing out of order.

"Sir," the maid called.

"I think it's under the bed," he lied. "We had a rough night."

Pulling his head out of the bathroom, he noticed the hotel phone had been knocked onto the bedroom floor. On a hunch, he walked over to the bedroom closet and yanked the door open.

Dodging her first swing with the desk lamp, he caught it on the second. "Baby, it's me."

As recognition seemed to overrun Remy's panicked gaze, he pulled her into his arms. "It's okay. It's okay," he repeated until her rapid, shallow breathing evened out. "We're okay."

Chapter Nine

Cutting their trip short, they had charted a private plane back to the States. Remy hadn't said much about the man in the elevator. Mistaken identity or jetlagged — past that, he couldn't get anything out of her. Years ago in college she had slipped once and referred to the guy as 'the man in black'.

Covered in sweat, Knox stood in front of the open refrigerator door and chugged orange juice straight from the carton. Since flurries were expected, he'd decided to skip his private gym around the corner. Instead, he had used the building's fitness center, pushing his body to the limit. He needed to work the alcohol out of his system.

Out of breath, he sucked down the last bit of juice.

Someone knocked on the door. Grabbing the remote, Knox turned on the television. The building's cameras appeared on the screen. Security downstairs had his list of guests who were allowed to enter the building. If he didn't know the person, they couldn't make it past the lobby.

His best friend Hawthorne Maze, aka Hawk, stood outside his door.

"It's open!" Knox pitched the empty carton into the trash.

"What the hell, man?" Hawk stepped into his condo. "My code to the private garage doesn't work."

"Sorry." He chuckled. "I forgot to tell you." Whenever Hawk made it to town, the hockey player crashed in Knox's spare room. He played for the Dallas Bucks, but after a couple of bad seasons, Hawk wanted a trade.

"Is this my eviction? 'Cause you're definitely giving me Vietnam flashbacks to my last relationship." Standing three inches shorter and fifty pounds heavier than Knox, Hawk was an enforcer on his team. Knox almost felt sorry for anyone who had to come up against the big guy...almost.

"Yeah, the thought of you seeing my baby naked brings about homicidal tendencies. It was best just to cut your code to the elevator before things got messy."

"It's true then?" Eyes open wide, Hawk's words came out as a hiss. "I thought... Well, it doesn't matter. When the hell did this happen? College? I mean...how? We were roommates."

"Look... It's complicated."

"I'm not Facebook," Hawk sighed.

Deep down, the man who cracked skulls for a living was a big softy.

"Do I at least get to meet her?" he asked in a petulant tone.

"Sure, but I need you do me a favor first." Chucking his thumb at the refrigerator door, he pointed to Remy's message on the chalkboard.

By the time their plane had touched down in Chicago, she had already filtered through a ton of work offers. *Do I want her to stay home? Sure. Do I think that will happen? Nope.*

"That's hella old school."

"Tell me about it. She doesn't have a phone. Pass me that." He pointed at the box on the end table. Knox had wanted to surprise her, but the iPhone hadn't gotten delivered until after she had left.

"This is getting stranger and stranger. What woman in this day and age doesn't have a phone?"

"Remy, that's who. Look… I need you to distract some execs from one of those fancy chick mags for me. The Mavericks' front office called an emergency meeting and I need to convince her to come with."

The beast put his hands to the sides of his mouth. "Paging Gavin Knox and his wife to the principal's office." He chuckled.

From what Knox could tell, his friend was finally loosening up, so he pitched the rest of his plan. "Not sure why, but yeah, I'm being summoned."

"Scoop her up on the way. I'm sure she'll understand."

Knox rubbed the side of his face, knowing full well that Hawk could read between the lines. "I need to persuade her first," he confessed.

"You're in the doghouse, huh?" he hooted. "And that shiny new toy won't cut it? Now I'm dying to meet her."

"No, it won't even crack the surface," he admitted to his best friend.

"All right, I'm in, but these fancy ladies may not be hockey fans."

"When has that ever stopped you?"

* * * *

Remy sat in the famous Chicago steakhouse, Gibsons, and listened to the woman wax a shiny spin onto their magazine's Executive Editor position.

As a gag gift, Knox had bought her a Hello Kitty watch several years before, but the joke was on him, as she rarely took it off. Controlling the urge to check it every five seconds, she trained her facial expression to mimic a state of mild interest.

"With your background and talent, M.M.C. Publishing believes you'll be a perfect asset to our catalogue."

"Your drinks." The waiter handed her a napkin with Knox's handwriting on it before setting the glasses down.

Women's restroom.

"Ladies."

Remy glanced away from the note to witness two professional women losing their collective minds over a flesh and bone *Games of Thrones* character.

"Oh my God, can I get a selfie?" one of them said.

Remy was pretty sure that the dude he resembled had gotten his head chopped off in the first season. She racked her head for his name. *Conan the Barbarian? Crap, I suck at this.*

"Hawk." He held out his huge hand. "I'm friends with your husband."

"From my understanding, you're the best one." She grabbed his big mitt and shook it. Tall and wide, Hawk's loose curls fell to his shoulders. His huge presence seemed to take up the entire room.

"Can you really say that at our age?" he asked.

"When you're the best one, you can," she confirmed.

Hawk broke into a huge grin that softened his intense features.

"If you guys will excuse me." Remy grabbed her purse and stood up. The rush for the lunch crowd had cleared probably twenty minutes before, but the restaurant still seemed fairly busy.

"Do you mind?" He gestured toward her vacated seat.

"Not at all." Positive Knox had put the man up to stalling for him, Remy hoped he'd promised his bestie something good in return.

She made her way across the main dining area and went upstairs. Remy pushed open the door to the ladies' room, where an 'out of order' sign had been posted.

"That took longer than I thought." Knox's deep voice caressed her as he leaned against the row of faucets.

"The restroom?" Remy twisted the lock on the doorknob before she joined him in front of the long mirror.

"This place is immaculate. You can eat off the floor." He picked her up and perched her on the edge of the sink.

Knox forced his large frame between her legs. "That shit I pulled on you in Barbados was emotional terrorism," he said, locking his deep blue eyes with hers, "and I'm sorry."

"What was that?" She cupped her ears. "I didn't quite hear you. Sooree." Knox rarely slipped into his Canadian accent, but she never missed an opportunity to make fun of him.

He turned his head to hide his smile. "Really, Remy? I'm trying to apologize here."

"Say it," she pushed.

"Fine." He leaned in close to her lips. "Requiem Bell, I am sooree that I put you in that fucked up position. I'm sooree that I gave anyone, especially you, the impression that I would ever cheat on you—"

She didn't wait for him to finish. Remy captured his lips between hers and sucked. Tense and tired, she needed an apology, but demanded sexual release more. "You smell good." Touching the tip of her tongue with his, she tasted mint.

Knox pulled away to nibble on her lower lip. "Never better than you." With a groan, he rested his forehead against hers.

Unwilling to let him ruin another sex-driven high, she kissed his neck, cutting off any deep thoughts he may have had. "What's our out time?" Remy licked the spot near the strong scent of leather and citrus that wafted from his skin.

"All the time in the world, babe." He pecked her on the head and reached underneath her wrap dress. After Knox pulled the sides of her thong down to the floor, he placed the lacy number in his pocket.

"This is seriously filthy behavior," she said in a heady daze, ready for him to feast on her.

"Just how you like it." He pushed her dress out of the way to kiss her thigh. "Whose pussy is this?"

Remy's breath hitched at his words. She inched her legs apart for him to see her wet slit.

"Say it," he demanded.

Wound tighter than a steel drum, she caved once he blew on her clit. "Yours, baby," she muttered, hypnotized by the devilish sparkle in his eyes.

"And don't forget it." Before she could respond, he attacked her pussy with missile-like precision. He closed his hot mouth over her swollen lips.

When he flicked his tongue over her clit, she sucked in a jagged breath. He manipulated her folds with tiny swirls. Pulling his mouth away, he blew warm air against her hot nub. Immediately she missed the comfort of his touch.

Knox slowly tapped her clit with his index finger. The methodical rhythm made her pussy ache. Reaching up, he worked his big hand inside her dress and shoved her bra out of the way to gently play with her nipple.

"Oh hell." She immediately bucked at the force he used to suck her. Dripping wet, Remy slipped her fingers into his hair to pull him farther into her crotch.

As he pushed his tongue deep into her core, she rode his face. Slow, mounting tingles ripped through her entire body.

"Come in my mouth, baby," Knox muttered into the slit of her pussy while he slipped his finger deeper into her throbbing hole.

Remy's climax exploded throughout her body, shattering her soul. "*Fuck!*" Gasping for air, she tried to steady herself. He held on to her thighs until she came down from her high

Swiping her cum from the sides of his mouth, Knox rose from his knees. "The front office called an emergency meeting." The mix of his breath mint and her pussy tickled her nose. "We have to cut this short."

Partially exposed in front of her husband, Remy sat in a lewd position on top of the sink with Knox between her legs. While she reached for his rock-hard cock, a devious smirk graced his face. Fumbling with the button on his jeans, she pulled down his zipper and shoved her hand into his pants. "They waited this long."

"My wife's presence has also been requested," he huffed, out of breath. Remy jerked his shaft up and down in the palm of her hand before she pulled him out.

"Ah, honey, getting off once isn't much of an apology," she cooed.

"So greedy," he muttered. Remy teased his enormous cock into the opening of her slit. Slowly he thrust his hips but didn't enter her. "This is important."

"Then you better hurry up and fuck me."

Without another word, he shoved into her.

Her breath hitched at the force he'd used. Filling her up with his rod, he held on to the sides of the sink.

"Your pussy holds me so tight," Knox grunted. Remy wrapped her legs around his waist.

While he sucked on her neck, he slammed into her over and over again.

"Fuck, fuck, fuck," she chanted.

As he battered her body from the inside, she threw her head back and groaned. In perfect harmony, they managed to rub out their orgasms at the same time.

"Knox…"

He clung to her body. They stayed intertwined in the bathroom of a four-star restaurant, sated and out of breath. Numb tingles shot through her arm from the weight of his huge frame.

"Huh?"

"We've got to go," she told him.

"Oh yeah." He pecked the side of her neck and worked his way up to her face to kiss her lips in a greedy, desperate manner.

"We smell like sex," she muttered.

"Yeah." Knox grazed his teeth over her lip. "That's why I picked such a primo restroom." He moved from between her legs, probably to keep the mess down to a minimum before he pushed his cock back into his jeans and pulled them up. "We can use some of these fancy things to clean up…" Towelettes, colognes and soaps were on a station near the sink. "So what's with the suits downstairs?" He snagged a cotton towel off the attendant's cart and turned on the faucet.

One of the strongest men she knew on or off the field, Knox hid his softer side with skill. Men displayed vulnerability differently than women. He'd be tense one second, clingy the next, but she'd honestly never seen him this bad. "I don't know. We didn't get to the meat of it," she lied.

"If you had to guess." He placed the warm cloth against her throbbing pussy.

Not sure what he wanted to hear, Remy shrugged. "Probably something to do with the latest matte lipstick color. Who knows?"

"Why aren't you telling me the truth, Heartbreaker?"

She chuckled at the nickname he had given her in college. "Let's deal with your job stuff first. We'll tackle my employment status at a later date." Unwilling to entertain a serious conversation half-naked with his hand between her legs, she kissed him on the lips. Deepening their contact, Knox pushed into her mouth with the tip of his tongue.

"Says the rich girl who doesn't need to work," he murmured once he'd nipped the bottom of her lip and pulled away.

Removing his hand from her crotch, Remy slid off the sink and dug in her purse for gloss. She needed to fix her face if she didn't want to model the 'just banged in a public restroom' look for the Mavericks' front office.

Chapter Ten

Portraits of past and present players lined the reception area of the Mavericks' stadium. A huge statue of their logo made of onyx and bronze emerged from the middle of the floor.

Intertwining her fingers with his, Remy squeezed the back of his hand. "You okay?" she asked.

"This Saturday school feeling has me tweaking." Regardless of his bad-boy reputation, Knox had never sought out trouble and he wanted to keep it that way. As the son of a politician he only had two options, and he always picked the Boy Scout route. Until Remy, of course. Knox would not only change his image for her, but also his religion.

"That's because you're Canadian. Don't worry, Supastar. I got enough detentions for the both of us."

"I'm sure you did." Knox smacked on a wad of gum with obnoxious intensity. They had managed to clean up in Gibsons' restroom in record time.

When they had gone down to the main dining hall, Hawk had seemed fine with the magazine execs and his iced tea. Knox had tipped the restroom attendant another fifty bucks and left his friend in the capable hands of two tipsy fans.

"Mr. Carter is ready to see you," the receptionist called them.

"Here goes me getting my nuts kicked in."

"So dramatic," she purred.

Knox opened the door with the honest-to-goodness belief that the only thing that would save his ass was on his arm...Remy. The Mavericks' owner and former player Bane Carter stood up from his desk to greet them.

As Knox stepped into the boss' office, the enormity of it took him off guard. A floor-to-ceiling window framed the Mavericks' entire field.

"What the hell, Remy? Not once did you say anything about being married—and to a football player, of all animals," Dahl Carter shrieked from across the room. With the office being damn near the size of a small apartment, he wasn't surprised they'd missed the owner's wife behind the bar.

"Dolly!" Remy screeched before she shook loose of his grip and ran to the woman. They screamed, laughed and babbled in some foreign language that eluded him. Seriously confused, he glanced over at his boss, who shook his head. Knox joined the football legend on the opposite side of the office.

"Sorry." Dahl, his boss' famous wife, laughed. An international chef, she had made a name for herself through rebuilding and rebranding failing restaurants. He had always wondered how these two strong personalities had clicked long enough to get married.

Bane didn't seem like the compromising type and neither did Dahl, but somehow it worked. "Remy here came into the restaurant where I was executive chef. What was that? Six years ago?"

"Yeah, when I first started traveling," Remy explained, carefully avoiding eye contact with him.

"Well, this sexy mama-jama came to my restaurant and liked my food."

"Loved," Remy corrected her.

As he soaked in the women's amazing beauty, Dahl grabbed Remy by the waist and squeezed her close. They were breathtaking. "That one is a Remy Bell original." Dahl pointed at one of the pictures behind them.

He turned toward the wall plastered with personal and professional photos of his boss' life. A framed magazine with Dahl on the cover sat front and center. She stood in the middle of a busy kitchen, with the blurry movement of her staff behind her. Antique colors of burnt gold illuminated Dahl at the stove. "Then she wrote this awesome article that led to my first television show. We've been friends since *forevah*. Oh, the stories we can tell."

A twinge of jealousy tugged at his gut. Knox shoved the irrational feeling down and plastered on a smile. "Wow, I would love to hear them."

"Did she ever tell you about the time we went running with the bulls?"

"The bulls, huh?" His voice pitched a tad higher at the image of her in Spain without him.

"Not actually running, per se, because we're not stupid." Dahl laughed. "But we had an awesome view from our hotel balcony."

Bane cleared his throat.

"Oh, that's my cue," she babbled sweetly. "My husband wants to rip yours a new one, and he doesn't want any witnesses around to see it."

"Dahl…" Bane sighed.

"Kidding." She guided Remy toward the door. "Good seeing you, Knox. Hopefully Bane isn't too hard on you." Remy tossed a wave over her shoulder. They left the office in a musical symphony of laughter.

"So, what's new?" his boss, a bigger and more ferocious version of The Rock, asked before he walked back to his desk. "Look… I don't really like to get into the personal stuff, but you're the face of the Mavericks." Bane gestured for him to take a seat. "Any reason why we didn't know about a wife until last week?" Without any discernible expression on his face, Bane sat down.

"Plenty, but I can't go into it," he said, hoping his answer didn't get him fired. The league structured the contracts in such way the players basically had to walk on eggshells.

"I heard that in one more season you're looking to get out. Now, if you were just some run-of-the-mill player, I would wish you good luck, but you're the best. We want you to stay in some capacity, even if it's not on the field."

"Shyeah right?" Knox said, shocked. He hadn't put much thought into his post-football life, but he found the soft offer nothing less than amazing.

"What is that, a Canadian thing?"

"*Wayne's World*." He brought up the cult classic.

"In other words, yes…Canadian." Bane swung his chair toward the stadium view. "We can work with a lot of stuff, but the public won't go for swingers or anything that messes with their hot dog-and-apple pie ways."

"It's not an open marriage and there's no cheating. I'm just an idiot. When I get the opportunity to clear things up, I will," Knox admitted.

"But that's not going to happen before the next season, right?" Taking a deep breath, his boss swiveled back around to his direction.

Sitting stock-still, Knox fought off the urge to bob his leg—a nervous tic he could never shake. Remy had encouraged him to remain cool before they'd arrived. "Probably not, but fingers crossed, eh?"

Bane chuckled. Most the guys got a kick out of his Canadian roots. Generally, they forgot he didn't share the same background, but every once in a while, he found a way to remind them.

"The team's publicity department can step in if you need them."

"My father got me someone," Knox confessed.

"Anybody I know?"

"Doris Petite."

"Hmmm, that's strange." Bane picked up a pen from his desk and tapped the ballpoint against the top of his Mavericks season calendar.

"Why?" he pressed, surprised by Bane's response. "I hear she's good."

"The best. We tried to hire her, but she has this thing about men. She'll only deal with women. I'm just surprised is all." Bane rubbed his hand across his face with a groan. "Okay, Knox, I'm going to trust you to clean this up, but I've got to tell you that it looks like America's favorite quarterback is a skanky ho who just cheated on a magical unicorn."

Unable to fully process that sentence, Knox cleared his throat. "Um...so, how are the kids?" A few years ago, Bane had inherited two nieces and two nephews. Apparently, the girls had done a number on the once-relentless linebacker.

"Yeah." Bane cringed. "I just heard how that sounded on playback. I may need lots of booze and a good poker game to wipe those words out of my vocabulary."

* * * *

Coasting on the remains of a mild Chicago winter, Remy found herself slurping down the best lemon Italian ice she had ever tasted. Dahl had taken her to a little hole-in-the-wall diner named Ed's Polish Sausages and Hot Dogs, a block away from the stadium. If Remy judged them by their Italian ice, then they were clear winners of the award-winning chef's imaginary junk food contest.

"When I saw you on the news last week with Knox, something occurred to me."

"We were on the news?"

"Not the real news. You know...tabloid crap. Alana loves it. There was this awesome shot of Knox helping you off the plane."

While her mind wandered, Remy tried to nod in all of the appropriate places. For the life of her, she couldn't figure out how her uncle's goon had tracked her to Barbados. She suspected he had been close throughout the years, but never in striking distance.

"Who's Alana?"

Dahl held her hand up in a time-out gesture. "You first...my stuff later. Anyway, it occurred to me you were the one to always call—and from a new number, no less. It only made sense, since you're the one who traveled all around the world, right?"

As smart as she was beautiful, Dahl would pick and pick at the same scab until it bled. There was no need to burden her friend with this mess. Remy sucked on her fruity dessert but kept her face impassive.

"Now that I think about it, I changed my number when I came back to the States," Dahl continued. "I emailed you and got short little messages back but nothing substantial…"

Remy only realized that she had completely zoned out once she no longer heard her friend's lulling tone. She looked across the table. Eyes soft with worry, Dahl was frowning at her.

"Honey, I consider us really good friends—two American black women making our marks on the world. But, I mean…" She yanked the knit cap off her head, releasing soft, bouncy curls, and leaned forward. "I thought the way you lived, hopping from one country to another, was amazing. However, the more I think about it, I can't help but wonder… Are you in trouble?" Dahl placed her hand on top of Remy's. "You can tell me if you are."

Remy took a hard swallow before she answered. She'd been on the run for so long that she'd forgotten what standing still felt like. "Well, I don't want to lie if I don't have to, so-o-o-o…" She patted Dahl's hand and went back to her Italian ice. Eying a group of teenagers' fries in the next booth, she considered ordering some. It would do her no good to have a nervous breakdown in a greasy spoon. *Got to keep that adrenaline up*, she coached herself with a small pep talk.

"Is it Knox? Because I can get Bane to kick his ass."

Remy damn near choked on her drink. Dahl's childish offer helped loosen the tight knot of dread that coiled in her chest. "No, not Supastar… Never him." Once she got down to the bottom of her cup, she sucked childishly on her straw.

"All right," Dahl said before she threw up her hands. "You're like a little sister to me and I love you, so I'm going to respect your privacy, but let me know if there's anything I can do. Since I started banging Bane Carter again, I have major pull."

"Again?"

"Oh yeah, it's a long story that involves four kids and a football team. If you want to hear it, you'll have to, at the very least, give me your new phone number." Dahl winked.

Chapter Eleven

Since Remy was far from a morning person, Knox usually let her sleep in. He nudged the bedroom door open with his foot. "Wakey, wakey," he sang. Clutching the Starbucks cup in one hand and the mail in the other, he walked to the bed.

"Come on, sweetie. Rise and shine."

She groaned and turned away from him. Kneeling by the bed, Knox blew the hot cappuccino smell in her direction.

"Leave me alone," she muttered, sinking farther under the covers.

"We've got stuff to do, and I have a meeting in less than a half hour, so wake up."

Remy's hand shot out from beneath the covers. She felt around until she made contact with his forehead, then shoved him.

"Dammit, Rem." She continued to muff his face with her palm until he got out of arm's reach of her smothering hand. "Fine." Putting the coffee on the nightstand, he grabbed the remote to the blinds. "One last time —"

"Get the hell away from me!"

He hit the remote, causing the slats to open. Bright sunlight penetrated the bedroom.

"Knox, I swear…"

Pretty black curls peeked above the comforter. She had always tied it up with a scarf in a complicated manner he couldn't figure out but found sexy as hell. He waited for her to emerge.

"The covers are next, babe," he threatened. "I don't want it to be like this, but you're leaving me no choice."

"Fine." Remy sighed.

As she stuck her hand up, he hurried to the side of the bed and handed her the cup of coffee. After a couple of sips, she flipped the covers down and poked her head out. "What?"

"Good morning." He grinned. Remy stared at him with a level of hostility he hadn't encountered in his fiercest competitor. "The first order of business." Knox held up her magazine. "Congrats."

"Oo-o-oh." When she opened and closed her hand in the give-me gesture for the *USA Today*, he tossed the newspaper into her lap. "I felt this was a good time to go over the rules again." His teammate's girlfriend, Lisa, graced the cover.

As a swirl of colors and people swam in the background, her smiling face stood out. *Pure elation.* "What's the problem?" she asked, obviously pleased with her work.

"For starters, Doug is a jealous psycho."

"Which means what? He doesn't want his hot girlfriend to be admired? Got it." While she sipped from her Starbucks cup, Remy scooted up the headboard and leaned against the wood. This early in the morning, he had hoped to catch her at a disadvantage. The next time, he would definitely leave out the coffee.

"Probably not by Mooch." He reached over and flipped the magazine around to face her. "This is the back of a huge football player. She is staring right at him with pretty much an 'O' face."

Remy tried to hide her smile behind her Venti cup, but failed miserably. "Come on, baby. There's no way Doug recognizes that look."

Despite his best effort to remain serious, he laughed at her. "Remy..." As he petered out, he dropped his head back, unsure how to get through to his wife. Out of all of the years they had been together, she had never hung around his teammates this long.

"Everyone seeing that picture thinks that she's happy to be at the festival. You're reading way too much into this," she assured him.

Knox shook his head at her flimsy excuse. "Okay, I see we're going to do this the hard way. This is your job." He held up the magazine. "Pithy little title, *Catch the Wave*, majestic picture, great story." He pointed at the byline. "Remy Bell right here. But this guy's job" — Knox chucked his thumb at his chest — "is to go on the field and avoid getting my skull cracked in." He approached the bed and took a seat on the edge of their California king. "Unlike you, I need a team. I can't do it alone."

"Doug's a roided-up hophead, taking his aggression out on her, and you know it."

"Let's just say the team has called for an intervention," Knox sighed. He knew better than to push too hard. She wanted to protect the weak—

everyone did — but there were limits to what they could do. "If we see something we don't like, then he's off the squad by any means necessary."

Remy closed her eyes and took a deep breath. "Lisa's family is in New York, which means she has no one here and no money of her own."

"He isolates her, I got it, but you're not going through the same thing, and —"

"The team's little plan to keep her safe will work for a minute. What happens when he finally tests dirty?"

The same thought had crossed Knox's mind, but he had his own wife to worry about.

"Modeling agencies will be interested in her after this, and Lashonda may even have a contact from her stylist days who can help —"

Knox held up his hand in retreat. "The wives have it under control. It's just the Mooch thing."

"We're not pushing it." Remy reached over and played with his hair. She knew he loved the feeling of her fingers against his scalp. It was distraction, plain and simple. The woman was crazy good at it. "I tried to crop him out of the shot, but the contrast of his body gives the picture depth, if you get what I'm saying."

"Yeah." He laid back against her. "It's that whole 'what you're seeing and what your eye actually has to focus on.' It's signature Remy."

"Okay, so what's next on the agenda?" she asked with enough humor in her voice to let him know she'd won that round.

He held up a square envelope. "I found this in the trash."

"Dumpster diving, Knox?" She plucked it from his hand and gave it a glance. "It's for some award ceremony."

"And you're being honored." He rolled onto his side to face her. "Why don't you want to go?"

"Hours in a formal dress with wilted salad? No thanks." A curl fell from the top of her scarf. She pushed it aside, causing the comforter to slip from her breast.

Instant hard-on.

"Besides, I bet you've been to a million of these things." She tossed the invitation near the trash. Of course, she missed and it landed on the wood floor.

"True, just not with you. The committee that runs this thing hunted me down. They really want you to attend." Unable to help himself, he reached over and circled her areola with his finger, which forced the bud of her nipple to grow taut.

"What are you trying to say, Knox?"

"Obviously, that I want to see you get an award." He pushed himself up and flicked his tongue against her nipple before he sucked the bud into his mouth.

Caressing the side of his face, Remy parted her legs under the covers just enough for him to get the hint.

"Don't you have a shoe signing that day?"

Rubbing his hand over the crotch of his shorts, he quickly did the math. He had a meeting with his agent and a potential sports drink sponsor in fifteen minutes. "I'll worry about that. Just take me out every once and a while. I feel like a dirty secret."

While Remy laughed at his joke—which held a ridiculous amount of truth to it—a dreamy glaze entered her eyes. If he drilled her pussy and manipulated her clit at the same time, ten minutes might put him in reach of an attainable goal.

"Dealer's choice," she huffed.

"Come on, babe." He shoved his shorts down. "I got a conference call in a few minutes." Since she always slept late, they had made a deal a long time ago that if he woke her up for morning sex, she got to pick the position. Naturally, her choices were always physically straining. "I'll owe you one."

Chapter Twelve

The Peninsula Chicago held a hall full of journalists and reporters dressed in their very best. The top stories of the year were rehashed and picked apart, while the people who'd relayed them were already three sheets to the wind.

Still stuck on her one-drink rule and surrounded by a table of strangers, Remy waited for Knox to join her. She wore a red, body-hugging, sleeveless number with a bejeweled neckline. Filthy sex in a swanky suite had enticed her to attend, but without Knox, the fantasy had evaporated.

Everyone seemed to know her name but not her face among all of these comrades and friends. She had always shied away from the camera, and by the time one of her pieces ran, she would have already landed at her next destination.

When her famous table of journalists laughed at the comedian on stage, she picked her vibrating phone up off the table and made her way toward the door.

"The whole reason why I'm here is because of you," she hissed without greeting him. "And you're not here." Not quite mad yet, Remy's emotions were edging in that direction.

"Sorry. It went longer than we thought. I've got Hawk with me. Do you mind?"

"The more the merrier, but he'll probably be bored. These people are pretty drunk."

The *Chicago Sun-Times* editor bumped into her. Remy barely dodged the woman's drink. "Sorry, honey." As a frosted-over glaze muddled her brown eyes, she bobbed left and right on her heels. "Don't I know you?"

Smiling, Remy pointed at her phone.

"Oh yeah, sorry," the editor mock-whispered. "But you look familiar…"

She turned away, hoping the woman had taken her not-so-subtle hint.

"We'll be there in ten minutes. Have they given out the awards yet?" Knox asked.

"You're that phantom girl. I had to make a million calls, because your uncle wanted to surprise you," the blonde woman guffawed before she slapped Remy on the shoulder.

"Excuse me?" Now *that* had gotten Remy's attention. *My uncle?*

"Congressman Brooks Richard… You're his niece. That sexy bastard was chomping at the bit to give you this award."

Remy scanned the large ballroom. Security details were stationed at all the exits. *How the hell did I miss that?* With her purse still on the table, she couldn't even make a decent run for it.

"Oh, look! He's arrived," the woman said.

As the congressman entered the stage and took the podium, the audience erupted in orgasmic applause. Salt-and-pepper hair covered the distinguished man's head. He had a perfectly manicured beard that helped him appear cool and youthful, according to an article in *Vogue*. Remy, on the other hand, knew better.

"Brooks is here," she muttered into the phone.

"Fuck, are you kidding? Can you leave?" Knox's voice had hardened.

"No."

"Stop the car!" he yelled, likely to Hawk.

"This is so exciting," the editor babbled drunkenly behind her. "He told me you've been traveling and thought this would be a good surprise."

"Find me," Remy said to Knox before she disconnected the call. Photos of her work appeared on the screen behind the congressman.

"What can I say about my niece, Remy Bell? I'm her only living relative, and although it's by marriage" — choking up, he held his hand to his mouth — "it feels like we're blood."

Remy wanted to throw something at the man or, at the very least, simulate gagging. Instead, she reminded herself to appear empathetic.

"For a very brief time, I was her custodial guardian, and I have to tell you that I'm beyond proud at what this young lady had to overcome. Remy reinvented herself into one of the most amazing storytellers of her generation." She caught the insult he'd gift wrapped into a crappy compliment. Sympathy and tragedy had made this man's career. Something big was on the horizon for him, which made it dangerous for her.

Different locations of her world travels graced the screen behind Congressman Richard. "The award for

Most Influential Photojournalist of the Year goes to my niece, Remy Bell."

Plastering a warm smile on her face, she snatched her purse off the table and approached the stage. Although he was silver-screen handsome, she couldn't understand why her aunt hadn't seen past the Southern charm of this psychotic predator.

Remy took the steps to the stage and accepted his hand. He pulled her into a tight embrace.

"Long time no see, baby girl," he growled into her ear.

Instead of sprinting to the nearest exit, she kept the same fake smile in place. "Thank you, Uncle Brooks," she said sweetly into the microphone once he'd let her go. "And thank you to the journalists who voted for me. I'm not in the States much, but when I am, there's nothing better than getting a surprise such as this...

"My husband is right outside, and I would like to thank Gavin Knox for holding down the fort, so to speak." Met with polite laughter, Remy went on for another minute before she left the stage with the congressman.

Applause followed them.

She scanned the room, checking for all the exits. Brooks must have sensed her hesitation, because he tightened the hold he had on her waist, commanding at a good six-foot-one-inch. His security team guided them backstage. The guard opened the door to a side room — where no one would be able to hear her scream.

* * * *

The background noise made it hard to understand anything, but he could have sworn the drunk woman had mentioned Remy's uncle.

"Brooks is here," she'd whispered into the phone, while Knox had tried to calculate his distance to the hotel.

"Stop the car!" he'd screamed at Hawk.

"What? Are you kidding? You can't wait five minutes to see her?" his friend had joked. "Give me a second for valet."

"Seriously, stop the car." Weekend traffic clogged the downtown streets. It would take Hawk another ten minutes to get them a couple of blocks away.

When they slowed down at the light, Knox opened the door and took off.

"What the hell, man?"

From everything he knew, Remy would have to keep cool to make it out of the award ceremony intact. Playing crazy only worked to the congressman's advantage. Knox's dress shoes slid across the sidewalk, but thankfully the salt on the streets allowed him enough friction to run. The bellhop opened the door to the ritzy hotel.

"The Hunter Thompson Awards?"

"Blue room around the corner and to the right."

Already breaking a sweat, he skidded around the corner. She wouldn't be in the hall anymore, but likely she'd be somewhere near the backstage area. Laughter poured from the award ceremony. Two guards stood in front of a door a little farther down from the banquet hall. Knox swiftly moved past the journalists and headed straight for Brooks' security.

Chapter Thirteen

The hotel's overflow of chairs and tables separated Remy and the congressman. She made sure to keep a ridiculous amount of space between them.

"Gotta tell you, baby girl, that you grew up to be a knockout. I'm glad I told Billy to leave that pretty little face of yours unmarked."

She'd always known that the congressman's goon had worked on Brooks' orders when she'd been attacked in college. "Billy has a bad aim. Maybe you should take your inbred cousin off the payroll."

"That mouth of yours... I nearly forgot how nasty it is." They circled one another. He wanted to throw her off balance, but the congressman had never posed a threat in person. Usually idiot relatives or employees did his dirty work. "I'm going to have to wash it out."

"Nice suit. What is that...Tom Ford?"

Brooks stood tall, arrogant and ready to inflict pain on any and all who were near him. He chuckled in that 'aw shucks' way that she despised. "Good eye."

"That's the thing I never understood." She shook her head. "How do you still get away with that 'poor country boy, pulling himself up by his bootstraps crap? Shit, Brooks, your worth is quadruple your state's median household income."

"What do the kids say?" He unbuttoned his suit jacket while throwing her a dashing smile. "Don't hate the player. Hate the game. Besides, your family is the gift that keeps on giving. Tragedy is an awesome drug."

"True," she agreed. Remy slipped her hand into the mouth of her clutch purse. "Aunt Valentine's 'suicide'." She threw up air quotes with her available hand. "Then my parents' carjacking. Instead of thinking you're a murdering psycho, your voting base just thinks you have bad luck."

"Don't forget how altruistic this white country boy appeared when he inherited a black orphan."

"A *rich* black orphan," she corrected. "And thank goodness I turned seventeen before that nightmare could officially take place."

"The honest truth of the matter? I believe you're the only reason I got voted into congress. That liberal bitch I ran against was hot on my heels in the election." He snapped his fingers. "And just like that, my tough-on-crime platform became the state's new bible. It was a shame your parents had to get their brains blown out to make that happen. Like I tell my constituents, you can't trust those urban areas."

When Remy had accused him of murder, he hadn't batted an eye. Related by marriage, he had used her sweet, quirky Aunt Valentine's personality to his advantage. It was obvious to anyone with more than two brain cells that the woman hadn't killed herself, but at thirteen, who would listen to Remy? Once her parents had finally caught on to Brooks Richard's bereaved widow act, their unfortunate deaths had soon followed. If he'd had them killed one month earlier, custody of their teenage daughter would have gone directly to him.

They stared at one another across the room. With that winsome political smile etched into his face, Remy knew she'd hit a nerve. The Bell family money had become the one thing he wanted but could never get. The maniac was pissed. He still had to shake that political stripper ass for a living.

"Remy!" Knox screamed from the other side of the door as a pit of dread dropped into her stomach. Then she heard, "Get the hell off me!"

"Lookey here, it's showtime," Brooks said.

"Nah, not today." She matched his sinister smile with one of her own. "We're going to walk out of here together, and you're going to tell those rent-a-cops to let my husband go."

"Why would I do that, baby girl? We're not playing that dummy's game. Was it football?" He jerked his thumb at the door. "We're in a different league, if you know what I mean."

"Exactly." The sound of a crowd forming outside filtered into the room. "The first casualty of this new shit won't be the quarterback of the Mavericks. I'm going for that idiot son of yours. What happens when your constituents find out you had to blackmail the little idiot's way into private school? And" — she held up two fingers on her free hand — "that he shares the same pill-popping habit as your whore wife." Remy opened her eyes wide. "Whoa, now that was a mouthful."

Brooks' genteel southern façade slipped from his face as he stalked toward her. She snatched her hand out of her purse and let him see the blue charge from her Taser. "Watch it, fam. It's going to be a bitch explaining why you have burn marks on those dimpled cheeks of yours."

* * * *

Rage coursed through his veins at the thought of Remy alone with the congressman. Knox tried to walk past the guards to get into the room, but they immediately blocked him.

"Remy!" Knox screamed. Not big on worthless conversation, he struck out. Connecting with the guy's chin, he body checked the guard on his left. Blind with rage, he didn't think words would help.

The biggest guy of the bunch tried to bring him down but couldn't get a good grip. Knox wrapped his hand around his partner's throat.

"Get the hell off me! " the guard shouted.

"What the hell?" Hawk rushed in. He tackled the guy Knox had been choking to the floor. Fists flew before the guards leaned against the wall, winded and out of breath.

"Both of you, hands on your head." Three officers stood in front of them with their guns drawn.

"Shit," he groaned

"Isn't that our freaking quarterback?" one of the cops asked.

"And that's the enforcer on the Dallas Bucks."

"These guys attacked us," the crybaby guard whined. "They're trespassing."

"What's going on here?" The middle cop dropped the muzzle of his gun toward the floor.

"An award ceremony. We're on protection detail for Congressman Richard."

"Who?" the cop asked.

"Not our state," another cop replied, while he holstered his weapon. "I'm not arresting our freaking quarterback for some yokel-ass congressman." The other cops followed suit and put their guns away. Hawk opened his eyes wide and shot him a 'what the fuck' glance. Knox shook his head. He hated that he had gotten his best friend involved in this mess.

"Get up, you two. Sorry about that." The police officer offered them a hand.

"They assaulted us!" the guard with the bloody nose complained.

"Well, I didn't see anything."

As they stood up, someone opened the door. "Gentlemen," Brooks Richard walked out of the room with a huge country-boy smile. "All this for little ole me?" On cue, a herd of reporters piled out of the convention hall and the congressman laughed, loud enough to draw even more attention.

"This man tried to bust down the door and attack you, sir."

"And the Chicago PD doesn't want to do anything about it." The congressman's security tattled like children.

Knox itched to hit them again.

Remy followed him out of the room a few seconds later. Keeping a safe distance between her and the congressman, she headed straight for him.

"Oh, I'm sure it was just a misunderstanding," Brooks said.

"Hey, can we get a selfie?" one of the cops asked.

Already in deep caca, Knox couldn't afford to piss off the cops. He jerked his head at Hawk for him to join them.

While they shoved in tight to take the picture, a reporter made her way to Remy. "What happened?" she asked. Most of the journalists already had their phones out, ready to record.

"It appears the congressman's security detail were Steers fans," Remy joked, loud enough for everyone in the hall to hear.

Once they were done, he wrapped his hand around Remy's waist and rushed them toward the lobby. "Good seeing you, sweetie. Call me for the holidays. We'll do Thanksgiving," Brooks called out.

Close to running, Remy stumbled slightly. He held her tighter and kept moving. Pulling her to the front, he shoved her into the revolving doors.

"What was that?" Hawk asked, as soon as they'd made it outside. Knox slipped off his suit jacket and placed it over her shoulders. "Gavin!"

"Keep walking." He wanted miles to separate them and the congressman.

"Are you going to tell me or is this shit going to be one big secret, too?" Hawk snatched Knox's arm back. He turned to swing, but Remy stepped in front of him.

"Don't you dare." She sniffed as tears filled her beautiful brown eyes to the brim.

For the first time that night, he took her in. She was stunning to a stupidly gorgeous degree, and he swallowed the acrid lump of bitterness in his throat and nodded. *Why does this evil man get to win?*

"I'm sorry," he said before he reached for her. Encasing her in his embrace, he took a deep breath.

"I'm sorry, Hawk." Knox glanced over his wife's head at his best friend.

"Yeah," the big guy muttered. "Call me when you can talk." Instead of waiting for his reply, the hockey player jogged across the busy Chicago street.

Chapter Fourteen

Two weeks after the congressman's ambush, Remy had fully reverted back to her old habits — paper currency, no credit cards and leaving the damn phone at home. She would never exit or enter the condo from the same doors, and she would make no habit-tracking stops. Unfortunately, the whole cash thing only worked if she went to an ATM to get money, not to mention that she could only make it a block from the condo before she needed a coffee fix.

"Sorry," she told the long line forming behind her in Starbucks. Pockets helped, but she had worn a dress that day. It was a cute denim number that became worthless on her journey to score a caffeine hit.

"Don't worry. I've got it," a well-dressed blond guy said. Since they were across the street from the courthouse, she pegged him as a lawyer.

"No, thank you. Really, I do have it. Who just wanders into a random Starbucks and thinks they'll get free coffee?" she mumbled, mildly annoyed that the man thought she needed to be saved.

"Someone who looks like you. I thought at least buying you coffee would make it easier to get your phone number." He grinned shyly at her.

"Sorry, playboy. She always leaves that shit on the nightstand." Knox reached over her head and swiped his iPhone across the card machine.

"Oh my goodness, it's Gavin Knox!" the cashier squealed.

Remy strolled over to the next counter to wait for her coffee. Thankfully, it was already done. Grabbing it, she headed for the door, not wanting to stick around for the *There Goes My Hero* sing-along that broke out every time Knox showed up in public.

"I hate your team," the guy said.

"Yeah, and my wife doesn't date losers, so it would have never worked." Placing his hand on her back, he pushed the door open for them. Double parked, he rushed her to the passenger side of his truck.

"What the hell, Supastar? He was just being nice," she complained.

"Sharks are cuddly and snakes are cute."

Remy fought against it but laughed in spite of herself.

"Now my turn. What the hell, baby?" He tossed Remy's phone into her lap once he got back into the SUV. "My mom called your phone. What's that about?" Since she couldn't come close to responding to that one honestly, she put in her code and checked her email. "Also, your noon appointment cancelled."

"And you answered?"

"Uh, yeah? How else am I going to catch you slipping?" He winked. "But the good news is you're stuck with me for the day." Putting the truck in gear, he moved into traffic.

"Presumptuous much?"

"Now, now… I can always take you back to that lawyer perv who was totally checking out your ass."

"And you know this —"

"Because I was checking it out first." Knox threw her a dazzling smile before he put his hand on her knee and squeezed.

* * * *

Knox had no idea how Remy had stayed two steps ahead of the congressman this long. He hated for her to be out of his sight for any extended period of time, but with the way their careers were set up, he had no choice.

Not having been assigned anything since the Wave Festival, she appeared to keep busy with meetings, emails and calls. The needling feeling that she had a plan that didn't include him messed with his chillaxed energy.

More often than not, they would be in the same room, but a ton of distance remained between them. Knox hated it. Deep in his thoughts, he pulled into the stadium parking lot. After swiping his keycard at the gate of the players' garage, he steered the truck around the twists and turns of the lot until he got to his private spot and parked.

"Why do you keep leaving your phone?" he blurted out.

"Do you want to rub out a quickie?"

They'd asked their questions at the same time, but hers had caught him off guard. He honestly never knew what to expect from his wife. Of course, random requests for public sex tended to be a hint that her muscles must have been tight — her euphemism for them to bone, not his.

"With you? Always. Now answer my question."

She had the first three buttons on her dress undone before he could stop her. "Sorry... I meant this minute." A lacy black bra cupped her awesome breasts. Reaching behind her, Remy had the dainty thing unhooked in seconds. Then she performed that wondrous magic trick where she pulled it from one arm of her dress and out of the other.

As Remy's brown tits bounced free, she threw her bra into the back seat. Knox licked his lips and tried to concentrate on something other than his dick.

"Oh...the phone." She hypnotized him with her slutty and completely sexy antics, and he almost let it slide. However, too much was on the line for them.

"In the past, you always used burners so they couldn't track you, right?"

"But you didn't buy me a burner." Remy popped the buttons to her dress.

Rooted to his spot, the horny teenager who squatted inside him wanted to dork out and pounce. Fancy lace panties hid the sight of her hopefully glistening pussy. Wild curls, pouty lips and big tits forced his mind to short circuit at the image of his hot wife in front of him.

Don't move, don't move, don't move, he chanted in his head. Once he touched any part of her, the conversation would officially be over.

"Supastar." Remy placed her sandal-covered foot across his leg and wiggled her fuchsia-painted toes. "You want to help a girl out?" She nodded at her panties.

"But if I bought you a burner…" He rubbed his hand over his crotch. His cock begged to be freed.

With a sigh, she lifted her hips and slid the lacy boy shorts down without waiting for him to assist. "It doesn't matter now. They can just stake out the condo."

Knox groaned. He knew he'd fucked up. Selfish and stupid, he hadn't thought that through. Since pretending to make his wife jealous ranked red on the idiot meter, he felt foolish. Unfortunately, he hadn't known how to get her attention any other way. Remy's lips were on top of his before he could encourage her to hop on the next plane out of there.

Ideally, he wanted her to stay with his parents, yet she hadn't stuck to that plan during their first year of marriage. Cupping the curve of her ass, he helped her over the console and touched the tip of his tongue with hers. She grabbed the crotch of his pants. "So what are your plans after this?" Remy whispered next to his lips.

Amused by her question, he smirked. "I've got clothes in my locker." She was probably worried about her pussy juices on his sweatpants, but he wanted to assure her that he couldn't care less. Grabbing the back of her head, he smashed his lips against hers to deepen their connection. Slow and sweet morphed quickly into a feverish energy.

As he lifted his hips, she made fast work of his pants. "Maybe you should turn around," he suggested. "I don't want to hurt you." His custom-built SUV accommodated him, but adding Remy to his seat would be one hell of a tight fit.

Several awesome scents wafted from her hot little body—a calming vanilla aroma drifted from her breasts, while a fresh-baked cookie scent swirled around her wild curls. Dipping his head into her round tits, he breathed in her sweet smell. She was sexy and lush in all the right places, and he needed her in the worst way.

"Nah, what's a little pain?" Remy lifted up her hips and slammed herself down on his cock. "Oh fuck!" she cried.

Unable to move, he sucked in a breath at the tight warmth that enveloped him. Dropping his head lower, he brushed his lips across her nipple. He wanted to feel it pebble against his tongue before he sucked on her hard bud.

"Hmm-m," she moaned. Knox shoved the left and right breasts together. Motor-boating, he went back and forth from one to the other. As he got lost in the snug fit of her pussy, every one of his senses pinged off the charts.

Up and down, she worked his cock. Grabbing a fistful of her hair, he pulled her head back and sucked on her neck.

Remy relinquished a strangled sob. He had heard this type of cry before. Soon, tears would follow. In the past he would have stopped everything, which made matters worse. If nothing else, Knox was a quick learner. He held tight to the back of her neck and pumped.

With very little room, he thrust into her. "Harder," she moaned through the tears. Remy arched her back, which brought a perfect breast directly to his lips. He sucked her nipple and pummeled her pussy at the same time. As her pussy walls tightened around his shaft, she screamed. The amazing friction knocked off his concentration, forcing him to explode inside her.

White stars floated in front of him. She had juiced his cock so hard that he couldn't focus. Clutching her tight, he tried to talk himself back into the worldly plane of existence.

"Hey," he huffed, still not completely in control of all of his faculties. Knox nudged her head up so he could peer into her eyes. He used his thumb to brush a tear away from her cheek. "What's going on?"

Remy's lips parted but no words came out. Glancing over his shoulder to the back of the truck, she slowly lifted herself off him. "Guards coming." She threw him a lopsided grin. "Try to be convincing." She quickly buttoned her dress and rolled down the window, probably to air out the smell of sex from the truck.

Slapped in the face by that high school detention feeling, he struggled with his pants and opened the truck's door to step out.

Chapter Fifteen

After a grueling gym session, he had taken solace in the four walls of his air-conditioned condo. Knox set his bag down and slipped off his shirt. Remy had a day-in-the-life interview with an indie rock band. As far as he could tell, she hated the confined structure of a schedule. Snagging his tablet from the coffee table, he headed into the kitchen and pressed the FaceTime button.

"Son," his dad answered. Knox plucked a Granny Smith out of the basket and popped the shiny green fruit into his mouth. Turning the screen toward the floor-to-ceiling window, he let his father see the coast, which was nothing less than awesome as the sun set on Lake Michigan. "*Très magnifique.*" The old man sighed wistfully.

"Papa"—he turned the screen back toward him—"why did you allow our marriage certificate to be released?" The question had nagged at him for months.

He had searched for someone to blame beside himself. At the moment, his father made the perfect target.

The kind man tilted his head to the side and peered into the screen. "Son, your stupid antics with the press put us all at risk. Did you forget I'm also a pretty big deal?"

Knox rarely messed up. Unfortunately, the one time that he had kept biting him in the ass. "I have to go to football camp... I'm leaving soon."

"Ah-h." His father pushed his glasses onto his head to rub the bridge of his nose. "Take her with you."

"I can't. No spouses are allowed."

"Remy is special." The old man chuckled.

"She is, but..." Four weeks was simply too long to be away from her.

"Gavin, you're brilliant and kind, but you tend to look the other way when you're displeased. You should have never played games with the tabloids."

Rolling his eyes, Knox groaned. Not in the mood for a lecture, he chomped on his apple.

"Eh-eh." Dad shook his finger at the screen. "You asked for it, so you hear me out. For years, Remy has sent her best photos to your mama. They made a game of it. She would guess which one the editor wanted. Well, once you decided to — what do the kids say? — test your wife's mob ties?"

"Gangsta, Dad," Knox corrected him. "Test her gangsta."

The old man chuckled. "She stopped contacting us entirely."

"Okay" — Knox held up his hand — "I got it."

"No, you don't. That's what I'm trying to tell you. We're her only family, and if she cuts off contact then poof!" He wiped his hands clean. "There goes the love of your life."

Knox dropped his head into his hands. The old man could always lay one heck of a guilt trip on him.

"That stubborn streak." Dad wagged his finger at the screen. "You got that from your mama. But," he said with a slight shake in his voice, "Remy's probably in more danger now than ever."

Brooks had transformed himself into a present-day Dorian Gray. No one would believe that the congressman was actually the devil.

"Face it and fix it. Understand me?"

"Yes, sir," Knox answered, automatically reverting back to his adolescent self.

"Now, how is my request for grandchildren going?" His dad flipped his glasses down and smiled at the screen.

"Working on it, old man." Hearing the sound of Remy's keys, Knox glanced at the door. She stepped into the condo.

"Is that Remy? Your mama wants to speak with her."

Remy shook her head in response to his dad's request.

"No, Papa," he turned his attention back to the screen, "I thought I heard something, but I was wrong."

"Tell Remy to call. *Bonne nuit*," Dad said goodbye. As he disconnected from FaceTime, Remy stepped into the living room.

First shoes, pants or skirt…then her magic trick with the bra. If Remy's clothes were discarded in less than twenty seconds, that meant she had a crap ton of stuff on her mind, none of which she would share with him.

"Hey, you got a minute?" he asked.

She kicked off her heels. The countdown had begun. "Ugh," she groaned. "Can it wait? I just need to hop in the shower."

Depending on Remy's mood, a shower might become the precursor to her mental checkout for the rest of the night. He had been lucky to get more than three words out of her during these episodes.

"It won't take long, babe."

Remy dipped her head down and twisted her long hair into a bun.

"We need to go shopping for some wheels."

"Why?"

"Uber's not that safe. And then there's the condo."

"What's wrong with this place?" Rolling her neck, she sighed, clearly irritated.

"Nothing's necessarily wrong with it. I just thought you would like to pick—"

"Really, Knox… This can't wait?" The last vestige of sunlight kissed her brown skin. Regardless of her bad mood, Remy glowed.

"Could you be less interested?" he blurted, unable to help himself.

Throwing him a death glare, she lowered her eyes to narrow slits and unzipped her skirt. "Considering this bra is slowly cutting off the oxygen to my brain, I probably couldn't care fucking less."

"Go." Finally fed up, he waved her off before tossing his apple core into the trash. *Easy two points.* "And why the hell does my mother need to talk to you?" he muttered to nobody but himself.

* * * *

The pulse from the showerhead beat against her skin. Remy leaned into the hard spray to soothe her aching bones. Six years' worth of running and hiding had finally sunk into her soul and weighed on her. Positive that she had caught sight of the congressman's idiot cousin earlier that day, she felt defeated.

Stepping out of the smooth granite bath cave, Remy snatched the towel off the rack and weighed all her options. Since the congressman still held a mighty powerful card up his sleeve, the thought to run had occurred to her. She oiled her skin before she whipped the towel off her head and dumped it into the hamper. Opening the bathroom door, Remy came face-to-face with one of the sexiest men she had ever laid eyes on.

"Want to start over?" While he held a glass of wine in one hand and a silky slip in the other, he graced her with a lopsided grin. "I mean, we can do this with you naked, but we both know how that will go."

Remy matched his smile and accepted the glass of wine first. Downing the moscato in record time, she nodded at the papers on the nightstand.

"It occurred to me that you've never bought a car before," Knox said, holding out the slip for her to take.

"What?" she smirked. "I just got out of the shower."

"Stop distracting me."

"No, to answer your statement." Done teasing, Remy grabbed the silky little number out of his hand, trading it for her glass. "I've never bought a car." While she put the slip on, he set the empty wine glass on the nightstand and grabbed the papers. As she twisted her curls over her shoulder, Knox guided her to the posh white rug, where they took a seat.

"Well, today's your lucky day, sweetheart."

His hard abs stood out under the dim light, the waistband of his sweats dipping low enough to show off his Adonis belt. Whatever he had planned, she hoped he kept it short. Sex always helped, and since she lived with a walking dick, a sexy distraction wouldn't hurt either. "A sporty convertible… Chicks love it." He held up the paper in front of her. "If you pick this, it sends me a huge message, because there's no way I can fit."

"Girly car, no Knox… Check."

He flipped to the next sheet. "Cute," he grumbled about the boxy truck, "and I can kind of fit in it, but this…" Clearly excited about that last one, Knox showed her a large SUV. "We can get it custom made for my petite frame, and I can drive it whenever you decide to get plastered."

"Because that happens often." She snorted.

"Just go with it," he said.

Remy reached for the printout of the truck Knox wanted her to get. "Okay, but silver." Pretty sure he had set her up to pick what he wanted, she caught his know-it-all grin.

"Next, this is the Loop. We live here." He showed her a picture of the downtown area, pointing at their building.

She rolled her eyes at his dramatics but let him continue.

"This"—he showed her a brownstone in a cute, quaint area—"is the Northside. It has more breathing room, awesome restaurants and it's kid friendly." He quirked his eyebrow at her in question, but she dismissed it. "And last…" Knox handed her a picture of lofts. "The Westside, an up-and-coming area with great buildings. I didn't do the suburbs, but that would be ideal for the dog and picket fence type of deal."

"How about...?" Grabbing her cell off the bed, Remy pulled up her cloud account and turned the phone in his direction.

"That's a pile of rubble," he said. She swiped to the next screen. "Wait a minute." Knox took her phone from her to study it. "Why do I know this place?"

"Try the next one," she told him.

He shoved back his hair as he shuttled through the pics. "What's going on?" The last shot showed the old farmhouse he'd grown up next door to in Canada.

"Your parents paid the down payment, and I pay the mortgage from my freelance checks each month."

"And?"

"Next picture." Remy nodded to encourage him on. "We break ground in the fall."

"How? I don't understand." He flipped through the photos of the blueprints. "You never take money out of the account. This makes no sense."

"It's your retirement gift. We worked on the layout—"

"*We?*"

"Your parents helped, but now that the cat's out of the bag, we can tweak it together... A summer home, I figured."

Lightning quick, Knox pounced. She didn't have enough time to react before he pinned her down and kissed all over her face.

"Get off." Remy swatted at him and laughed.

"Admit it. We are the bestest, most awesomest couple. Why do you fight it?" His sparkling blue eyes seemed to dissect her as if she were a mathematical problem he couldn't quite figure out.

"Because I don't want to lean too hard on you," she answered.

"But I love it when you do." Knox kissed her on the lips, moving against her mouth in a slow, torturous manner. "Full disclosure... I just left the gym." He lowered himself down to suck on her neck.

"Why would that matter? We're just talking, right?"

Shoving her legs apart with his knee, he slid the strap of her slip off her shoulder and kissed her erect nipple. "We are," he huffed against her breast. "But now I'm going to do it while fucking you."

Chapter Sixteen

The Chicago streets were crowded with people. It was a perfect day for a walk. Remy found herself turned around near the river. She had somehow gotten off track and was late for Lashonda's photo shoot. A startup magazine wanted to hire Remy for their head editor position. Without a firm commitment either way, Remy had left for her next appointment.

"Catch an Uber!" Lashonda hollered on the phone. "This is my first shoot in years and I'm nervous."

Remy had scored the stylist a cushy freelance job for the cover of a magazine. She'd promised the football wife she would help her out. Of course, she needed to get there first. "Hold on. I'm a little turned around is all."

"I'll drop a pin."

"No," she said, more harshly than she intended. "I'm at Franklin and Wabash. I just need to get to Orleans." Remy always kept the location feature on her phone off.

"Okay. Do you see the bridge? Keep going and it turns into Orleans. That will put you right by the Merchant Mart. I'm a block away from there."

"Got it." The streets were jam-packed. She had to wait for the light to change. "Give me five minutes." Who knew stylists were more temperamental than their freaking clients?

"These people are like hella professional and I've been in mommy mode for a good minute, and—"

"Girl, breathe! Shit." Less concerned about her surroundings and more worried about Lashonda's freak out, Remy let her guard down.

"You never should have come back, bitch," he growled before he snatched her by the arm and shoved her into oncoming traffic.

"Remy, Remy!" She could barely hear Lashonda over the hard blare of a car horn.

* * * *

As the emergency vehicles blocked off the intersection, Remy sat on the curb. Blood slipped down her knee.

"I saw him push her. I mean, he was right there," the kid who had yanked her from the clutches of a Nissan bumper babbled to the cops.

"That leg looks like it needs stitches." The EMT knelt beside her and pressed gauze against her knee. "Do you understand?" He held up his hand. "How many fingers do you see?"

"I'm refusing medical service. Is there something you want me to sign?"

He sighed. Probably not the first difficult person he had dealt with today, Remy felt positive she wouldn't be his last. "It can get infected. I suggest you let us take you to the hospital." The paramedic got up and went to his truck.

"Honey, you should listen to him," a woman near her said.

Remy felt dizzy. The crowd seemed to close in.

"Hey! Hey, I'm her husband!" Knox's voice carried over the symphony of voices. After a few seconds, he appeared directly in front of her.

While she held the gauze to her knee, Remy raised her hand for Knox to help her up. The EMT returned with the medical release on a clipboard. "We recommend that she go to the hospital," the guy addressed Knox instead of her.

Freakin' snitch. Obviously, he figured the QB would be easier to convince.

"Babe…"

"No," she said in a flat tone that left no argument as she scribbled her name on the sheet. Remy handed it back to the ambulance driver before she hobbled toward Knox's truck.

"Some guy pushed her. I saw him!" the college kid who saved her yelled. "Tell them."

"I'm not sure. There were a lot of people," she lied. "But thank you."

"Aren't you Gavin Knox? Hey, everyone, it's Gavin Knox." His attention quickly moved on to the football star.

"Shit," he muttered. The cops tried to keep the emerging crowd back. "Hey, man, I appreciate your help. Call the front office and we'll see about getting you some tickets." Knox cut a good path through the crowd.

"My friends are going to shit a brick!" the kid yelled.

"Ma'am, did you want to file a report?" the officer asked. Knox had parked in the bike lane. Amazed that Supastar had managed to pull that totally illegal move off, she rolled her eyes at his arrogance.

"No," she told the cop as Knox held open her door and helped her in. "I'm sure it was just an accident."

"Quarterback," the EMT yelled. He threw a roll of tape at him. "You're going to need that."

Once they were alone in the car, he opened him mouth, but she promptly cut him off. "The shoot is a block away."

"Remy…you can't be serious?"

"We're not fighting about this."

"But—"

"Alone." She stopped him from any further argument. "Just drop me off, alone."

She felt his heated stare but refused to look at him. Putting the car in gear, he pulled away from the curb. The drive took less than eight minutes.

"How did you know where to find me?"

"Shonda called. She heard a car horn and screams. She couldn't get you back on the phone. Speaking of which—"

"Dead… Roadkill… The cell is permanently part of the street now. Sorry."

He gently pulled her chin in his direction. Up until that moment, she'd done a pretty good job of avoiding eye contact. The sadness, pain and disappointment telegraphed on his face would chip away at her already weakening resolve. She simply couldn't afford it.

"Why don't you head up to Ontario for a few weeks—or Ottawa? My parents are there." Knox continued to hold on to her chin.

Instead of answering him, she grabbed the passenger-door handle, and leaned over to place a quick peck on his lips. "I'll call you when I'm ready."

Remy snatched the tape out of the console and hopped out of the truck. Limping into the building, she hurried into the elevator. She wrapped the gauze around her leg, finishing before the doors opened.

"Are you okay? Knox called me," Lashonda greeted her in an exaggerated Nicki Minaj outfit. A Playtex mini dress and a big blue wig would probably be a hard sell on anyone else. Strangely enough, it looked anime-hot on the curvy-ass woman.

"A little nick," Remy lied. As they stepped into the swanky production company, the football wife gently took her arm and helped her into the studio. "No biggie." She hopped into the dressing area.

"Okay, girl, cut the shit." Lashonda closed the door behind her. "I heard what that man said. *'You never should have come back, bitch.'* What the hell?"

"Uh-h." Remy lowered herself onto the stylish chair that had no padding whatsoever. The cute crap made every ache in her body intensify by ten.

"Don't lie. I've got three kids, so I'll know." Lashonda pointed her long, multi-colored nail in her direction.

Buying herself some time, Remy dove into her purse and rummaged around for the pain pills she'd received for her ribs. Her leg was on fire. She probably should have gotten stitches. The last time the congressman had acted this erratic, people had ended up dead. After she found the bottle, she unscrewed the childproof top and gestured at the basket of water on the table.

"Did you tell Dre?" Remy mumbled over the Vicodin-ibuprofen mix.

"Not yet." Lashonda reached for a bottle and twisted the top off before handing it to her.

"Good, don't." Remy popped the pill into her mouth and chased it with the water.

"Girl, did you rob a bank?"

"Why?" Remy asked her. "You want in?" They stared each other down.

"Yeah." Lashonda broke first with a lopsided smirk. "Mama needs a new pair of shoes." They fell into peals of laughter. Once Lashonda petered out, she snagged a jacket off the dressing rack and tossed the designer number at her. "Since you're obviously not going to tell me anything, let's get to work."

Chapter Seventeen

Out of his mind with worry, Knox had requested an emergency sit-down with his illustrious boss. While he stood outside of Bane's office, he weighed his options. A gun probably wouldn't work for her. He knew how to shoot but Remy didn't. Also, the odds that an assailant would wrestle it away seemed likely.

"My man." Andre, who walked into the reception area half asleep, reached out to slap his hand.

"Sorry if I woke you," Knox told him.

"No big. Had a late night… We set up a mock testing for my new vodka at Moe's. You know I'm all about that retirement life."

"Correct me if I'm wrong, but that's not for a couple of years, and Moe's crowd is bordering on dead. Why didn't you have it at Murphy's Pub?"

"It's too trendy with all those damn lights. Besides, Moe's has the best vibe."

Bane opened his office door. "Not one star player but two. I can't wait to hear this," the owner said drolly.

"Get in here." He flipped his hand toward the room. *No warm and fuzzy teddy bear today.* Knox really hated to spring this on Bane. "What do you want?"

"This is kind of a GM conversation, but—"

"Then go have it with him." Bane took a seat behind his desk. Even though he had dressed down in jeans and a T-shirt, it didn't make him appear any less menacing.

"For camp, I need Remy with me."

"No-o-o-o." Bane directed his attention toward his desktop screen. "Good talk."

Rubbing at the knot of stress that had formed in back of his neck, he slid a glance toward Andre. Instead of stepping in for an assist, his teammate strolled toward the wall of photographs. *Abort mission.* His subconscious screamed for him to let it go, but Knox had to see this through.

"It's an emergency."

"When Doug came up here, it was *muy importante,*" Bane replied. "A couple of other people who I can't even remember needed the same crap. The answer to them and you is 'no'."

"Then I'm out."

"What?" Andre and Bane exclaimed unison.

"She won't be sa-a—" Knox stumbled over his words. "I just can't leave her alone."

Leaning back in his chair, Bane sighed. "It's only four weeks. How about she stays with Dahl and the kids?"

As Andre plopped down on the couch, Bane threw him the stink eye. The running back doubled down and snuggled farther into the cushions.

"Won't work," Knox admitted.

"I need a compromise, Canuck. There's no way I can justify you bringing Remy." Bane continued to type on his keyboard, not paying him the least bit of attention.

"Okay. Well, I'll have my attorney contact the league to bang out an exit strategy."

"What the fuck is your deal?" Bane roared. He stared at him with a stormy contempt that made Knox believe he wasn't above punching one of his players.

"Hey, hey." Andre held up his hand. "Canada here is the freakin' easiest. Knox has never been a problem. If he says he needs Remy around, I believe him."

"Look… I handed him a solution. Unless he wants to tell me something that will change my mind, we're done talking."

"Maybe your solution sucks," Andre countered. "She's a journalist. Give her a press pass."

Knox's mouth fell open. He had an education from a Big Ten university with an undergrad degree in finance and he still couldn't come close to Andre's genius. A simple solution he hadn't even considered had come out of the hungover running back's mouth.

"This will cause a shit-ton of problems with the team." Bane leaned back in his chair with a groan.

"We'll handle it," Andre told him.

"Can I at least get a heads-up?" Bane asked. "What's the mystery?"

For years it felt like he had carried the weight of the congressman around his neck. Knox really wanted to tell somebody. However, to place other people in the path of danger simply wasn't an option.

"Hawk said it's pretty bad and we can't help."

Knox slid a glance at Andre, who finally sat up.

"Moe's. Remember I told you I went last night?" The bar was a second home to Hawk. Knox had been so consumed with his life that he'd completely forgotten that his best friend's season had ended. "He's knocking out a contract with the Northern Royals."

Crap! Apparently Hawk had got traded. Since Andre loved to needle him, he fought to keep his expression neutral.

"What the hell am I listening to right now?" Bane complained. "Days of Our Hockey?"

"Does she get the press pass or not? 'Cause I got my own shit I need to talk to you about."

"Yeah, well, I don't want to hear anything, and I mean *anything* from your teammates," Bane groused. "Now you go." He tossed his hand in the running back's direction.

"My boy is retiring after next season. I want to pick his replacement."

Steam practically poured from atop Bane's head. After a good few minutes of pure silence, he glared at Andre. "I'll think about it."

"My bad... I think I said it wrong. Juan is inconsistent and will only win us first prize in the shitty arm contest. Nothing personal, but I don't have that much time on the clock to watch him fail. Besides, I'm the one who recommended Knox, so-o-o..." Andre stood up. "Trust me." On his way past, the running back tapped him on the arm, signaling for them to leave.

Throwing a polite nod at his boss, Knox followed him out of the door. "Uh, so you wanted to piss Bane off?" he asked, once they were clear of the owner's office.

"Nah... I don't want management to get any bright ideas. From what I hear, no one's been looking for your replacement, and I'm not about to watch my last season circle the drain because of Juan's ass."

As they hit the doors to the garage, Knox put his hand out. "Thanks for coming."

Andre slapped his palm and gave him a half hug. "Not a problem. You're like a brother to me. But seriously, I saw Hawk that night of the award ceremony and he was pretty shook."

Lost in the ocean tide of his own mess, Knox had completely forgotten about his best friend. "I need to talk to him." Rubbing the stubble on his face, he wished he could shake loose that crushing ball of dread squatting on his chest.

"Yeah, I guess. White-boy problems." Andre walked to his car.

"Dude, you know he's half black, right?"

"What?" The running back held his hand to his chest in mock outrage. "And he plays *hockey* for a living?"

Every once in a while, Andre would feign mock ignorance on Hawk's decision to play on the ice instead of the turf. "Black people do play hockey," Knox corrected him, confused as to why they had to keep having this conversation.

"Dammit, Knox, I don't like liars." Andre hit the alarm on his car. "And right now, you're lying to me."

"Dre—"

"Don't." He hopped into his sports car and rolled down the window. "It's going to take a minute for me to get over this betrayal." He chucked deuces out of the window with a cackle. "Peace."

Chapter Eighteen

Humid heat swept the university's field. With three weeks of training camp down and one to go, Remy sat in the stands with the other journalists. The players had practice from dusk to dawn. She wondered why management had picked the worst time of the year for such a strenuous workout.

Since the players' day had been scheduled down to a tee, Remy spent all of her time with strangers. Light banter back and forth with the other reporters kept her mildly entertained. She couldn't have any real conversations, considering she needed to keep her distance. The quarterback and his wife seemed to be a bigger story than their defense for next season — or even the strategy for their offensive line.

Bronzed from the sun and soaked in sweat, Knox made his way to the water jugs.

"He never even looked in this direction before you showed up." Without a lick of grace, the old man pushed past the other journalists in the stands. Remy shaded her eyes from the sun, amazed by his determination to reach her. He had almost fallen twice.

"Dammit, Art," one of the guys said. He'd probably crushed the poor man's toes.

"It's not like you don't see all this sexiness." Art bumped him in the face with his pregnant belly. "Now move." He fanned away the young intern who sat next to her. Popping a squat in the freshly vacated spot, he shoved out his hand. "Art Newhouse. That jackass you married calls me Artie and the shit stuck."

"Should I pretend like you don't know me?" Remy ignored his hand. "Or go straight in on you like I have a bone to pick?" Since Art was nothing but a lovely mess, she didn't bother to hide her smile.

"Considering I was the one to dig you up, it honestly could go either way."

"Damn, Artie, I'm not dead." Remy left off the 'yet', since the congressman had set his sights on her like never before.

"I didn't mean to imply such. You got any quotes for me, gorgeous?" The old curmudgeon snatched a pen out of his shirt pocket, ready to write notes across the byline of his own newspaper. *Such a professional.* Remy snorted.

"Everything we say will be off the record, sweets," Remy fired back. After Knox slung the ball down the field to the rookie, he locked eyes with her and frowned.

"This is already pissing him off. Coming up here might have been worth it," Art noted with a grin.

Remy decided to keep an open mind. She totally understood why he rubbed Knox the wrong way.

"Tell me, beauty queen. What do you see in him?"

"Is that a real question, Art?" she chuckled. "Jill!" Remy shouted at the intern he'd misplaced a moment ago. "Why do you think everyone wants Knox?"

The college co-ed turned from the wire fence that separated them from the players. "Do you want the 'three peppermint schnapps-down' type of girl talk or the 'I'm among colleagues and need to be polite' answer?" Jill pushed her square glasses that had slid low back onto her baby face.

"I mean, besides the obvious," he muttered. "He's nowhere near as smart as you, and that arm has got what? Three…four more years tops."

"Real talk," Remy ignored Art and encouraged the intern to let it rip.

"Have you ever seen that meme where the cat has its ass tooted in the air?"

The men groaned.

"Or that girl who has her legs wide open, pointing to her crotch, where you can come get it," she continued. "Like…get it in."

"Geesh," Artie said.

"That's why women shouldn't be allowed in men's sports," one of the reporters complained.

"Gross," another guy shouted.

"Not what I meant." Art grunted while he hung his head. "College was years ago, and that hot jock bit gets old after a while."

"Bullshit!" Jill pointed at the men in the front row. "I call bullshit. Do you know how many conversations I've walked into where you misogynistic assholes demean and reduce women to sex objects?" She addressed the whole section. "News flash… Your wives aren't watching this shit because they care about team stats or throwing averages. Hell no! They want to know what that dick does—and you guys are too stupid and arrogant to see it."

Unbelievably tickled by the college co-ed, Remy clapped and cheered for the girl.

"Jill!" Everyone on the bleachers turned their attention to her boss, who had entered the bullpen. "May I have a word?"

"Shit, that's my third strike," she hissed.

"What was the second one?" the quiet chick from *Fox Sports* asked.

"The color commentary guy… I threatened his future firstborn if he ever accidently brushed against my tit again."

The woman nodded. Remy couldn't tell if the *Fox Sports* reporter agreed with Jill or the decision to fire her, since she went back to her Sudoku puzzle fairly quickly.

With her shoulders low, the intern trailed her boss on the walk of shame. "Don't worry about it, Jilly," Remy called out to the intern. "I got you."

"Thanks, Remy, but you write your own ticket. I need someone with sports outlets' pull."

Way too bright to be relegated to intern for a craptastic station, Remy refused to let the girl be reduced to sports roadkill. Considering she had instigated the hell out of that highly entertaining meltdown, she felt responsible.

"Did you forget who I'm married to?" Remy nodded to the field where several players, including Knox, were staring at the press core bleachers.

Jill squealed. Most of the men plugged their ears and groaned. In probably her best imitation of Jude Law in *Breakfast Club*, the soon-to-be-ex intern pumped her hand in the air before she left their little bird box area.

"So, he's basically Superman, and you're what, Lex Luthor?" As if nothing had happened, Art picked up their conversation.

"That's a strange analogy. No, it's more like if Superman decided go dark and bang Harley Quinn." Most of the reporters nodded in agreement. "Did you know Knox has his BA in finance?"

"Yeah, yeah." He poked his lower lip out.

"Now, let's start over." She put her hand out. "Remy Bell, and you're going to run down everything you know about football to me."

A hint of a grin crossed his grumpy face. "Why can't you ask Dudley Do-Right?" The bleachers laughed at his Canadian diss.

"Asking a football player about football is the worst kind of pain." They turned their attention toward the field. Knox threw up his hands in a WTF move. Remy laughed. He had no idea what they were up to, which probably really ticked him off.

"Is it me or is he pissed?"

"Well, it is super-hot out," she admitted. "But don't act like it wasn't your goal to make him mad when you plopped your ass down."

"True." He grasped her hand within his sweaty mitt. "If teaching you football keeps that expression on his face, I'm in." Art shook on it. "What do you need to know?"

* * * *

An epic summer storm raged outside. Remy grabbed her red Solo cup off the nightstand and sipped the lukewarm riesling. After studying her football notes for close to fifteen minutes, she had finally given up. The team had a week left until the end of camp and she still didn't have a good angle on a story. Her focus majorly sucked. The press had waited for hours in the hot July sun for a few stingy sound bites from the players. Front office had needed to put her and Knox on notice about fraternization more than once.

Instead, she pulled up an article about her uncle. For years, Remy had investigated and studied the congressman's rise to power. Always on the edge of illegal activity, he dipped his toes into the pool but had never quite jumped into the deep end. Even if she found the smoking gun on Brooks, he would find some way to wiggle out of trouble. At this point, she would need an avalanche of evidence to bury him.

While rain battered against her hotel window, she went through news stories and television clips of dear old Uncle Brooks. It was a long shot, but nevertheless, she searched for that needle in the haystack. Sliding farther underneath the cool hotel sheets, she studied the congressman's latest endeavors.

The hard rhythm from the rain helped to quiet her thoughts, and Remy felt her anxiety ramp down a notch. Thunderstorms didn't usually bother her, but every so often they would remind her of the night her parents had been killed. Two cops had arrived at her private school to hand her over — signed, sealed and delivered — to the politician. Remy had known better than to leave with them. In the middle of one of the worst spring storms, she had snuck out of her dorm room and had been playing keep-away from her uncle ever since.

Exhausted, she closed her eyes. A boom of thunder startled her upright. Lightning from the storm flashed outside the patio window.

As a slight sheen of sweat kissed her skin and a flutter of panic spread through her chest. She must have fallen asleep.

"Remy." Knox stood at the end of the bed.

"What the hell?"

"The power's out all over the city. You forgot to engage your security lock," he huffed, out of breath. "I just ran up five flights of stairs. I tried to call, but —"

He crossed over to the patio doors and slid it open. "It's hot as hell in here." When he turned to face her, the taut muscles on his face relaxed into a lopsided grin and he kicked off his shoes. "This place must not have a back-up generator."

"What are you doing, Supastar?" Although slightly groggy, she couldn't miss the moonlight showing the twinkle in his eyes.

"Well, you know, since I'm here…" He pulled the end of his shirt over his head. "We can catch up on some snuggles. I've got a few minutes before anyone will notice that I'm gone."

"When did cuddling require you to be naked?"

"Everyone cuddles naked, baby," he said matter-of-factly. Already out of his shorts, Knox flopped onto the mattress. "Damn, this bed is small."

"Maybe you're just huge."

He grabbed her ankle and tugged her down to him, kissing her on the lips. The instant warmth of his mouth caused twisty flutters of heat to tickle her insides. He tried to guide his cock into her opening, but after three weeks, Remy wasn't up for a missionary quickie.

"Dealer's choice."

"Come on, Heartbreaker. My muscles are sore and I only have a few minutes," he whined. "Getting back on campus will be a lot harder when the power is back on. I'm already risking one hell of a fine."

"Dealer's choice." Remy traced her tongue along the bottom of his lip and deepened their kiss before she flipped on to her side.

"Dammit," he hissed. Positioning himself next to her opening, he nudged himself between her legs. "First off, I love and hate that you sleep naked." As he placed sweet kisses along her spine, he grabbed a chunk of her curls and moved them away from her neck. "Seeing you every day and not being able to touch you"—he slowly maneuvered the tip of his rod into her slit—"is agony."

Gently biting her neck, he started to pound her pussy from behind. When he reached around to caress her nipple, Remy moaned.

"Fuck, this pussy is good," he growled.

Determined to hold out a little longer, she eased away from the tingles of a good orgasm and laid the front of her body flat onto the bed.

"Ba-a-a-aby," Knox groaned before he slapped her on the ass. "You're killing me here." Climbing on top of her back, he slipped his huge hand between her and the bed and slid his cock back into her pussy.

While Knox used one hand to balance his weight, he manipulated her clit with the other. Left breathless, the pounding her pussy took sent shockwaves of pleasure throughout her entire body. A feral scream erupted from her core.

Slapping the palm of her hand against the headboard to stop her soul from shattering apart, she continued to holler.

He stuttered out indecipherable words before he laid his head on top of the back of hers. His heart beat wildly in his chest, and Remy felt it pounding against her back. "Don't run," he begged. Without waiting for a reply, he kissed her neck and climbed out of the bed.

As the storm finally slowed to a crawl, Knox went into the bathroom. Sex drunk, she nodded off. When she heard the door creak, she opened her eyes.

"Why would you think that?" After he had reduced her to a wet, vibrating mess, she didn't think he could flip the mood that quickly.

"Canada with my parents." He stood in front of the window, allowing her a good shot of his muscled ass. However, his side profile made her want to grab her camera. Chiseled cheekbones, strong jaw... Mix all of this with his intelligence and kindness and none of it was an expected match.

Since the moment her parents had died, Remy had insulated herself within a world that would protect her. College had become a fortress between her and the congressman. She'd used her sorority sisters as buffers. However, her chance meeting with the quarterback had changed her perfectly constructed life. Falling for Knox had forced her to let her guard down, which had allowed her uncle a foothold into her world.

Their fairytale had soon twisted into a rushed marriage born out of panic and fear, not to mention a miscarriage that she'd never told Knox about. Unfortunately, those high-octane emotions still fueled them. Stay and die or run to fight another day. The cliff-jumping adrenaline never ended. It was a matter of time before he grew tired of their out-of-whack lifestyle.

Lately Remy had felt the weight of their relationship on her shoulders. If she didn't give the football god that farm and kid fantasy, the whole affair would soon be over.

"Knox, that's not what…" she tried to tell him, but her explanation died on her lips.

"Don't break my heart," he said softly, "again."

A lump formed in her throat, and Remy swallowed hard. The congressman got to win while her world spun out of control.

"The night we met, I remember you running and looking back. Was someone chasing you?"

A physical badass, Knox was one of the sweetest men she had ever met. "Supastar—" she attempted to stop him.

"At the time, all I knew was that the girl of my dreams had fallen right into the palm of my hands."

"Uh, well, you kind of grabbed me." She softened at the memory.

"It took a minute to get it, but you would have done a hell of lot better without me. I mean, shit…" He rolled his shoulders before turning to face her. "This is not your thing, and I shouldn't have brought you back. It was selfish. But please, just do me a favor and stay… One season with you in the stands is all I want. We can get security to follow you around, or I can cut the season short…take the contract hit. But we can—"

"Stop. I'm not going anywhere," she promised. Usually honest to a fault, Remy tended to avoid conversations that forced her to lie.

"Good." He snatched his discarded clothes off the floor. "Now what's up with you and the old man?" His abrupt change in topics threw her for a loop.

"Who…Art?" She wound her curls around her shoulder, happy to move on to safer ground. "He's cool."

"That hideous human being has bashed me my entire career. Are you really cozying up to the enemy?"

"Don't exaggerate." She took in the sight of the sexy man putting his clothes back on. Abs, guns…hell, Knox even had amazing thigh muscles.

"Tell that hack to keep his old man cooties away from my wife." He yanked his shirt over his head. "Also, what is the deal with you and my mom? Why do you keep dodging her?"

"Huh?" Caught off guard, she tried to train her face. Soon the prime minister's wife would send the Canadian Mounties to hunt her down. "I texted her," she told him. The message had held no substance, but she needed to keep the woman from showing up unannounced. "How much trouble will you get into for this?" The lights hadn't turned back on yet. Knox still had a fighting chance to get onto the university campus sight unseen.

"A fine, maybe."

"High or low?" She offered him the game where they would bet on something.

"Five thousand, up to twenty-five thousand dollars. You go," he told her.

"Nope, you."

"First, I will not be getting caught, but if I do, no more than ten thousand."

"Twenty-five thousand," Remy picked. "They'll want to make an example out of you, and I need money."

"Really? For what?"

"Not sure yet… A business maybe." Knox took care of their finances and did a hell of a job, but Remy wanted to try her hand at investing.

"Since you're going to lose, no problem," he agreed.

"And what do you want?"

"For you to take out your IUD, as soon as possible."

"Oh." Barely able to keep herself safe, she didn't want to rain on his parade. Remy had no plans to provide the congressman with another blood relative to go after.

"Deal?" Kneeling across the bed, Knox leaned toward her.

Another lie? Oh well... She would feel bad about it later. "Deal." Remy met him halfway for a sweet peck on the lips.

"Now put the security lock on the door," he told her once they'd parted. With sparkling eyes that danced in the moonlight, he tugged on her hand for her to follow him. For a split second, Remy wanted to tell him about the miscarriage, but she shook it off. Maybe once the smoke cleared, she would let him know that having a baby might not come so easy.

Chapter Nineteen

Camp had finally ended and Knox wanted to sleep for days. During those weeks, the women had planned a lot of activities and Remy hadn't gotten to experience any of the fun. Celebrating their return, the wives had thrown a mixer for her. Apparently, they wanted to recreate the college co-ed atmosphere, to show Remy what she had missed.

It was an awesome gesture that ultimately put him in his teammates' crosshairs. These men had gone for weeks without sex. However, Dahl had extended the invitation, which meant none of the wives would turn down the Mavericks' owner. Everybody's blue balls simply had to wait.

Knox opened the door to Moe's, a crusty blues dive located in River North.

"Why?" he asked Andre, who sat the bar. The place was a freakin' eyesore.

"Because Dahl pours a mean drink, which means I need a ride to get Lashonda." Andre devoured the basket of buffalo wings in front of him.

"That doesn't answer my question." Remy had carpooled with Lashonda. Of course, it had never occurred to him that the designated driver would need one herself.

"My car is too shiny and beautiful to be decorated with puke."

"Ah, there it is… Pure selfishness."

Andre chuckled, with no shame. "Besides, Moe's is the best. These appetizers…" He whistled. "Good music — and no one bothers us here."

"Man, you trust this food?" Knox wondered why the room appeared dusty. Pictures of all the old greats — Muddy Waters, B.B. King, and John Lee Hooker on stage — covered the walls. Ten senior citizens sat around the tables to enjoy the band, who, at first glance, appeared half dead.

Andre tossed the last bone into the basket and got up. "On to the next topic at hand. Things have become seriously awkward and I'm going to need you two to kiss and make up. We gotta pick up the girls in about an hour."

Confused, Knox squinted at him until Hawk stepped out of the swinging doors from the kitchen. As the situation finally dawned on him, Andre grabbed his drink and left them alone.

The hockey player nodded before he went behind the bar. As he was close with the owner, Hawk would often pass the time slinging drinks on the weekends.

"Hey." Knox held out his hand and the big guy reluctantly slapped it. "What's going on?" Since dealing with the congressman, he hadn't had time to add their bro mess onto the pile of problems. A part of him felt bad, but not bad enough to seek Hawk out.

"Not much. Just got traded to the Northern Royals."

"Congratulations, man."

With a slight smile Hawk nodded his head. "I'm pretty excited about it. I wanted to call you, but…"

"Yeah, well, I'm happy for you regardless." Knox bounced his leg up and down. He had a lot stuff on his mind.

"Still not going to say anything about that shit with the congressman?" Hawk poured the beer on tap and slid the mug across the bar.

"It speaks for itself, doesn't it?" Accepting the dude form of a truce, he grabbed the drink. Knox could have been wrong, since Hawk often held a mean grudge, but he took a chug of the frothy brew and sighed. After all those weeks in camp, a good hit of cold beer did wonders for his state of mind.

"That last summer before your senior year, we were supposed to go to Cancun, but you canceled at the last minute. And after senior graduation, you bailed on the apartment." A year behind him, Hawk had had to fend for himself once Knox had gotten drafted. "I was lucky enough to get another scholarship to cover your cost, but even that was bullshit, wasn't it?"

No matter how crappy it made him feel, Knox deserved this guilt trip. Hawk had grown up in the foster care system and they had met at hockey camp. The two had been inseparable ever since.

"Regardless of what you or your parents think about me, I'm not a charity case." Hawk grabbed a mug and swiped angrily at it.

Strong on pride, Hawk would have freaked if he'd ever found out that his family had funded his scholarship.

"Look, man… You're like a brother, and…well, since you're probably making more money than me, feel free to pay me back," Knox offered.

Hawk chuckled, which helped. The big man had always been a hard nut to crack. "Do your parents know?"

Toying with a coaster, he twirled it into a circle. "I had no choice but to bring them in," Knox admitted. "If I could do one thing different, I wouldn't have involved them."

"And Remy?" Hawk casually leaned against the bar.

"Cards on the table?" Knox asked. "As long as I'm with her, nothing else matters."

* * * *

The last time Remy had had a true girls' night out was college. Somewhere between drinks, karaoke and the tarot card reading, she realized Brooks Richard had changed the trajectory of her entire life.

What if her parents had never died? What if she had been left beaten for Knox to find? And the miscarriage she still hadn't told him about… After so much time had passed, it had become easier not to say anything. However, he kept bringing up that huge Canadian family he wanted.

Standing in the kitchen, she studied the wine in the cooler. Not officially on the safe side of completely drunk, she felt the effects of the alcohol begin to dissipate. Remy didn't want to lose the foggy haze. She struggled to get the wine opener into the cork.

"Hey, so I was thinking— Whoa!" Fresh out of the shower and clad in his favorite pair of sweats, Knox grabbed the bottle out of her hand. "You didn't get smashed enough at Dahl's?"

Instead of responding to his question, she waited for him to open it.

Twist, pop… Everything is so easy for Knox. She chuckled at the rhyme and held out her glass, but he only poured a small amount into it. Tilting her head to the side, she glowered at the handsome man.

"Trust me, babe. You're going to be feeling this in the morning…" Pouring the glass well over the halfway point, he passed it over to her.

"What do you say to staying with my parents for the season?"

Fuck no! But she couldn't very well say that. Not being in any condition to verbally spar with Knox, she chugged her glass of wine in the most lady-like manner that she could manage. Stuck in a lose-lose situation, she did the only thing that came to mind and grabbed a handful of his crotch.

"So is that like a 'yes', you're going to do what I ask for a change?"

Remy set her glass down and slipped her hand into his sweatpants.

After a few good strokes of her hand, his dick grew from a semi to rock-hard in a matter of seconds. Since Knox kept his face blank, she couldn't figure out if he wanted to go further until he reached over and thumbed her exposed breast. Earlier she'd put on one of his tanks that simply didn't fit.

Remy bit her lip and lowered her eyelids to peer up at him. She was going for seductive, maybe, or she might just look like a drunken mess. Either way, she wondered if he would fall for this little act.

Knox had seen her tipsy but never drunk. Obviously, he wanted to capitalize on this current mood and get her to spill her innermost thoughts. Sinking down to her knees, she grabbed the sides of his sweats and pulled them with her.

"What are you doing, Heartbreaker?" he asked with a husky tone. She didn't bother to reply. Instead, she kissed the tip of his cock that sprang free. Pre-cum coated her lips before she opened her mouth and took in his large rod.

"Shit!" Choking his length in her fist, she bobbed up and down on his cock before she pulled him out. With a smacking pop, she licked the underside. "Play with yourself," he demanded.

Remy rolled her eyes toward his to see if he was kidding. The dreamy glaze of bliss written across his face told her that he was serious. Before she sucked him back into her mouth to throat-fuck his cock, she leaned back on her heels. Spreading her legs wider, she slipped her finger into her folds.

"Mm-m," he moaned. "Come here. Let me slide into that pussy."

"Nuh-uh," she mumbled over his shaft. Passionately sucking him faster and faster, she twirled her tongue around his tip and squeezed his length in the palm of her hand.

"Oh shit, baby." He grabbed the back of her head and fucked her mouth.

"Remy, I'm about to—" She choked his rod harder in her hand. "Argh!" He coated the back of her throat. "Fu-u-uck." As she allowed the rest of his seed to dribble onto her chest, Knox huffed out a breath.

Wiping her mouth with her hand, Remy stood. "That was awesome, honey." He gathered her into a close embrace. "And I can't wait to remind you tomorrow that you sucked my dick like a fucking porn star, but you didn't say... Are you going to Canada or not?"

Chapter Twenty

The dog days of summer in Chicago were humid as well as suffocating. Of course, her hangover didn't help. She was barely coherent when Knox dragged her to the clinic. For a subpar medical facility, it wasn't that bad. Remy had seen worse. Unfortunately, all clinics sported that gray film of despair.

"Want to grab a bite before we go to Jake's?" Knox played with the pump on the blood pressure machine.

"Nope." Beyond nauseated, she couldn't think twice about eating. She had woken up with a head full of twist braids accompanied by one hell of a headache. *How the hell do I keep getting different hairstyles?*

The only reason she wasn't still in bed was because Knox had blackmailed her into a follow-up visit to the clinic that had checked her out when she had arrived in the States. It was a completely useless endeavor, as far as she was concerned. Bruised ribs were the least of her problems. Positive that she had caught sight of the man in black on their way there, Remy worried about what he would try next. Since there were too many people around for him to get away with anything, he probably just wanted to keep her off balance with his presence.

"I've got to say that I've never seen you this jacked up before." Knox chuckled. "I thought these girls' nights would be this obnoxious pain in my ass, but I got the best surprise when you got home."

"Huh?" She plopped her sunglasses on her head to scowl at him. "What the hell are you babbling about?"

Knox stopped toying with the machine to cross over to the exam table. Placing his forehead on of hers, he rubbed their noses together. "You gave me the best blow job of my life, Heartbreaker." Slowly and sweetly, he kissed her on the lips.

"No-o-o." Remy felt her jaw and twisted it around. She had wondered why it had felt crazy sore this morning.

"After literally ripping my spirit from my body…" Sitting up, he dramatically put his fist to his mouth and pretended to cry.

"Knox, I swear," she threatened him through gritted teeth. The urge to hit him rolled through her body.

"Then the most wonderful, beautiful thing happened… You swallowed."

"What the hell?" she squeaked. "And you didn't stop me!"

"Why would I?" As he erupted into a deep belly laugh, she punched him on the arm. "Tell me, baby. Was this legit the first time you've been drunk? I mean, I truly scored big last night."

"Shut up, Knox." Before she could hit him again, someone tapped on the door.

As the doctor entered the room, Knox piped down to annoying giggles.

"Good news…" the doctor said, "your ribs look great." The tiny woman held Remy's X-rays in her hand.

"Hey, Doc, how long after she takes out her IUD will it take for us to become preggers?" Knox asked in a half-joking, not-joking way.

"Us?" Remy snorted.

"I'm pretty sure you need me," he shot back.

"Somewhere around six months to a year. Uh, let me see…" She glanced through the files in her hand. "It looks like you had a miscarriage, so you might want to get the IUD taken out sooner rather than later. That way you can tackle any fertility issues that can arise while you're still young."

The room immediately filled with suffocating tension, and the doctor glanced between the two of them. "I'm sorry, did I — ?"

Remy hopped off the exam table and plastered on a tight smile. During her last visit, she must have mentioned the miscarriage on the medical checklist. "Uh, thanks. Do I need to come back for anything else?"

"No, no, you're one hundred percent. Try not to be late for any more flights, okay?" The doctor opened the door. Remy tried to follow her out of the room, but Knox reached around her and closed the door before she could walk out.

"What the absolute fuck?"

* * * *

Ripe anger poured off Knox in waves, which was almost worse than the hideous August heat. *Almost.* The telltale signs that his level of pissed-offness had spiked way past red on the angry meter were his clenched jaw and bulging forehead vein.

In an attempt to keep up with him, Remy doubled her steps.

"Gavin!" She'd wanted to wait until they left the clinic to talk. However, she didn't mean until next week. She hated the silent treatment. *I fucking loathe it, actually.* "Dammit, Knox." Running around to the front of him, she forced the giant off the busy sidewalk. Her five-foot-nine-inch frame compared against his gigantic six-foot-six-inch stature must have been laughable to anyone who saw them.

Totally avoiding eye contact, he rolled his baby blues skyward. He couldn't even look at her. "It was a couple of weeks after we were married. I mean, I was already pregnant because we were banging like…" She couldn't even get a complete thought out. "Shit."

"When you got beat up, right?"

Clearing her throat, she pushed on. "We thought it was better to tell you later."

"We? My parents know?" He finally looked down at her.

"Yeah. I needed their help with the insurance because Canada has that good stuff." She tried to joke, but his creased forehead told her he wasn't in the mood. As the muscle in his jaw worked back in forth, his whole face drew tense. Remy cleared her throat and pushed on. "Everyone agreed that we shouldn't affect your draft year—"

"Fuck!" He grabbed the sides of his head. A couple of people stopped to witness their favorite quarterback's meltdown. Holding her position, Remy trapped him against a brick building. A tiny bunny manhandling a lion probably seemed weird, but she didn't care.

Knox had every right to be mad. Purely worn out, she dropped her head onto his bicep. "Trauma to my uterus caused it, but I should still be able to carry a baby to term."

His muscles tensed underneath her head. Remy could hear his heart beating wildly in his chest. He finally wrapped his arms around her. "Senior year, right?"

"Yeah." They stayed locked in an embrace for some time. The wave of rush hour traffic changed from a trickle to a full-on tsunami of people.

"How many kids can you see us having?"

Having avoiding the topic with him in the past, she had never put much thought into it. She raised her head to read his expression. Knox had always believed the congressman would eventually give up, but Remy knew better.

"To tell you the truth, I've never really thought about it. Maybe two."

"Cool. We'll shoot for four. That way I'll be sure to get three." As if that were the end of the discussion, he kissed her on the head.

"Uh, how does that work?" She tried to pull away from him, but he held tightly to her.

"Easy… You have to make it up to me."

"Not with a whole damn kid, Knox — or two, with your weird-ass logic."

"Hmm-m-m." He finally loosened his hold on her. "It seems fitting." He held his out hand. "So, are you ready to go? We don't have to stay at Jake's long."

Remy opened her mouth to dispute the fact that he couldn't negotiate humans that came out of her vagina, but she decided to let it go for the time being.

"Uh, yeah." She intertwined her fingers with his. "Let's eat something greasy to knock out this hangover." They maneuvered their way back into the busy Chicago foot traffic.

"Usually drinking gets rid of it." He winked at her.

"The major head you got last night should hold you for a while."

"Said no dude *ever*," he replied sarcastically. "Besides, who knew you had porn star skills like that? I just want to try them out again to make sure that wasn't a one off."

"Seriously, Knox, shut it." Too tired to hold her throbbing head up straight, she leaned against his arm. "And never — and I mean *never* — bring this up again."

* * * *

Murphy's Pub had a line around the corner. Since Jake's grand opening, plenty of tourists stopped by in hopes of spotting professional football players. Since the place was packed to the gills, the team went upstairs to the VIP area. Sleek booths were set up for more room against the wall. Since the team had demanded privacy, security had roped off the balcony area.

Loud beats battled with the voices of the customers. Remy dearly wanted to go home, but she had to wait for the cake. All the wives were supposed to sing happy birthday to one of the players, but she was too hungover to remember which one.

"Thanks to you, I got another shoot," Lashonda screamed over the music.

"That was all you, sis."

"If you hadn't gotten me the job, I wouldn't have been able to prove myself." Lashonda gestured with her drink in Knox's direction. "So, um, are you two okay?"

His teammates laughed and chatted all around him. Knox sat on the fancy leather bleachers, not bothering to engage in conversation with anyone.

"He didn't get much sleep last night — and now with the new season…" Remy lied.

"Sure," Lashonda said, before taking a sip from her drink. "And don't forget that shit going on with you two." The banging beauty whipped out her phone in perfect Perry Mason Exhibit A dramatics and scrolled through a gossip blog. It showed the fight they'd had outside less than twenty minutes ago. "I would say by that 'tiny girl blocking big football player' move, which I am a pro at" — Lashonda patted herself on the back — "you done fucked up."

Quarterback Fights with Estranged Wife in Public. Is Divorce Imminent?

Remy shook her head. "Where was this dude hiding, the gutter?" Blow-by-blow pictures of their fight had been recorded for public consumption. The blog speculated what the problem could be, since she had appeared only months ago.

"Yeah, you would be surprised at the stuff those toads get of me and Dre," Lashonda admitted. "And at strip clubs, no less. Freakin' soul suckers… Isn't anything sacred?"

"Don't worry about us." Remy handed her phone back. "We're good. But if we could speed the festivities up, 'really good' could happen a lot sooner."

"On it." While Lashonda took off toward the kitchen, Remy made her way to Knox, who sat with a far-off gaze. He continued to nurse the same beer he'd received when they'd walked into the pub. She knew he wasn't still mad at her — he had always gotten over stuff fairly quickly — but a melancholy edginess emanated from him.

"Hey," she said.

The corners of his lips turned up into a warm smile. As the hard expression he wore softened the tense muscles in his face, the spicy leather scent of Gavin Knox filled her. He brought her lips to his, kissing her with a long and punishing neediness she had never seen before. Remy put her arms around his neck and melted into his touch.

"I love you," he whispered in her ear once she'd pulled away. "And I should say it more, like every day, but I'm just afraid that —"

"I'll get spoiled." She laughed. Often, she would hear him utter those words after sex, during that weightless moment where she teetered on the edge of hard sleep.

"That you're not real," he continued to whisper in a husky, sensual tone. "And that you'll somehow slip through my fingers."

Studying his face, Remy wondered where the hell all of this had come from.

"Remy," Lashonda called her, "the cake is ready."

Knox raised his eyebrow. "Home after this?"

"Hell yeah." She pecked him on the lips one last time before she faced the wives to join them.

"Hey," she asked Allison, "is there a private bathroom up here?" Afraid her period had started a little late, she didn't need the paparazzi to get another embarrassing shot of her on the way home. Allison pointed to the side door. "Thanks," she muttered. Remy veered away from the group and pushed the long door handle. If she hurried, she could slip back into the crowd near the end of the song.

The door shut behind her. Seconds too late she realized that the stairwell led to the exit. That idiot Allison had lied. Locked out, she tried to knock, but no one could hear her over the thundering sound of music in the bar. Giving up, Remy went down the narrow stairwell that led out of the building, but thankfully someone opened the door behind her. A stream of music and laughter flowed toward her.

"Thank goodness, I thought—" Her words died in her throat.

"Hey, baby girl. I've been waiting a long time to finish what I started." The man in black practically flew down the stairs at her.

Chapter Twenty-One

The hypnotic beat of the music annoyed him to no end. From the moment they'd walked in the pub, Knox hadn't wanted to be there.

"Hey, man" — Andre passed him a bottle of beer — "you look like you could use something stronger."

Knox accepted his second beer of the night and sucked down the nutty, bitter taste. It was some craft crap, which Jake had named after one of the Maverick players. Each player had a special beer to honor them.

"Taste like shit, doesn't it?" Andre asked with a wicked grin.

He wanted a normal-tasting brew but didn't hold out much hope of getting one at this particular pub. "Yep, whose is it?"

Andre chuckled then tilted his head in the direction of their relief quarterback. "This beer should be labeled weak as fuck, like that fool's arm."

Knox nodded in agreement.

"Okay, what the hell is wrong with you? That was funny," Dre asked.

"Nothing. Tired, I guess." The wives came out with a ginormous cake covered in sparkler candles. He scanned the group for Remy but didn't see his wife. "Shonda?" Knox threw his hands up.

"Just saw her a second ago."

"The side door," Allison offered a little too gleefully for his taste. "She thought it was the bathroom."

"Why didn't you stop her?" Lashonda barked. "You know it locks once you leave."

Panicked into action, Knox jumped from the bench.

"I'm not her keeper." Allison cackled. "So, she'll have to get in line with the posers. It's not a big deal."

"Hey," Mooch asked, most likely reacting off his frantic expression, "you want me to help look for her?"

"Check out front." Knox hurried to the side door at the far end of the room. Jake warned them that if anyone left that way, they would have to go around to the front of the pub.

Knox flung open the door and was instantly dipped into complete darkness. A keyhole of light from the bottom of the stairs showed a flurry of shadows.

Without his mind truly comprehending anything, he charged. Holding her own, Remy fought, but slipped back a step. The man grabbed her wrist and shoved something into her side.

She gasped, a harsh sound that echoed into Knox's head, vibrating over and over again.

Before the sick fuck could use the knife a second time, Knox body slammed him into the wall. He felt a sharp sensation of pain—a slice into his arm—but it wasn't enough to stop him. Smashing the man over and over again, a whimper from Remy snapped him out of his rage.

The minute he took his eye off the goon, the man fled out of the side door.

"Don't," she murmured.

"I'm just trying to help," Mooch reassured her. He tried to reach for her again. "I need to stop the bleeding."

Jagged pieces of everything Knox had told him over the last few weeks had apparently gelled together into the perfect picture.

As Knox pulled his shirt over his head, he knelt next to his wife. Remy's beautifully brown eyes went languid. "Go get your car," he told his teammate calmly.

"She needs an ambulance!" Mooch screamed, damn near hysterical.

Knox pressed his shirt to her side. "Get your fucking car, *now*!"

For weeks she had slipped him a little information here and there with off-the-cuff conversation that had made no sense. Research for a story, he'd thought at the random non-sequesters she would lay down, but no, Remy had prepped him subliminally.

"Chicago County?" he asked. She nodded slightly and sucked in a breath. There were several hospitals closer, but they needed one that couldn't be bought off by the congressman.

A crushing weight of pain seemed to squeeze the air out of his lungs. Knox stamped down the wave of panic that wanted to take over.

Minutes that felt like hours went by before he heard Mooch's horn. Knox scooped her up with no effort and kicked the side door open. The kid ran around his truck to help him put her into the back seat before he smooshed in next to her. "Go, go, go!"

* * * *

Everything had blurred together into an eyes-wide-open nightmare. How long it had taken for them to arrive at the hospital or who had taken her away from him, he couldn't say. Caked in her blood, Knox stared at the emergency doors that had closed.

"Sir, we're going to need you to fill out this paperwork."

"Garcia needs to see my wife," he muttered the words Remy had told him to say. When they'd arrived, he'd explained to the nurse that she needed to see this doctor but didn't think they'd heard him the first time. "Uh, Dr. Rosa Garcia."

The nurse stared at him for a moment then blinked herself back to the present. "She's already been contacted, sir. You should grab yourself a seat."

Mooch tugged at his arm and led him away from the desk. "I appreciate this, but you need to leave," Knox said.

"Man, I'm not going anywhere," Mooch said.

"Yeah, you are. Don't worry. The police will be here soon," Knox told him.

"Don't you want me to give my statement?" the rookie asked.

Annoyed that he had to think about anyone other than his wife, he snapped. "Look, man... You don't have the best track record with the cops. I won't be able to save you. God!" He grabbed the side of head with both hands. "Shit, I'm doing a really bad job saving her."

"But why would I—?" Mooch began, but suddenly stopped. "Okay, okay, but if you need anything..." He nodded before he stood up and walked to the ER doors, almost colliding with two guys who looked a lot like plain-clothes cops.

"Gavin Knox." The two men headed straight for him. They weren't in uniform, but he recognized that flat tone and dead expression. The men offered their names, but he didn't hear them. "We need you to come with us."

"Now, why would he do that?" Doris, his father's fixer, stepped in behind them. Even though she was dressed down with jeans, she still held that same intensity that she had when they had met months ago.

"Argh. Petite, this isn't media blitz. His wife was almost killed and we need answers."

"Yeah, there's a conference room down the hall. If you think for one second that you're about to take my client on a perp walk, you're crazy."

"Hold on, hold on, hold on. Don't make this a thing. We just want to ask him a few questions." The gruff one smiled insincerely. "Besides, we're the good guys."

The publicist guffawed. "This is not my first rodeo, sweetheart, but if you want to do this the hard way…" Doris pulled out her phone.

"All right." The serious one, who had silently stared daggers of hate at Knox, stopped her. "After you." He signaled with his hand toward a set of double doors.

Chapter Twenty-Two

After thirty minutes of the same questions asked in different ways, they had finally let him go. Knox had wanted to wait for Remy to get out of surgery, but Doris had strongly encouraged him to leave the hospital with her.

In other words, she had threatened him that she would quit again and let those dirty cops take him to the precinct if he didn't get in the car. He didn't care about that, but once Doris implied that she would leave Remy hanging, he reluctantly followed her out of the hospital.

"Not for nothing," Doris said, "but I really think you should have gotten stiches for that arm." While bad cop and worse cop had pretended to listen to him, a nurse had bandaged his biceps.

Clueless about how the night had spiraled this far out of control, Knox got into the back seat of Doris' chauffeured Lexus SUV. "How did you know to" — dizzy, he tried to quiet his nerves — "come here to find us."

"The nurse. 'Dr. Garcia' is a code. She contacted me. Thankfully, I wasn't too far away. After your trip to Barbados, Remy came to see me. She knows the plan. Now it's your turn. If you deviate from it then we'll be forced to part ways. Got it?",

He nodded, unable to do much else.

"Congressman Richard will be running for President in the upcoming election," Doris said.

"Fuck!" He choked on his anger. Big, racking coughs shook his body. "She knew, didn't she?"

"Remy? Yeah, she suspected. My team looked into the matter and found it to be true, along with everything else she told us."

Knox badly needed to break something. He hit the button to lower the window. After a few deep breaths, he managed to push down the jacked-up adrenaline that had surged through his veins.

As his life fell apart, he pulled his head back into the truck.

"Better?" Doris asked. She never took her eyes off her phone.

"Not by a long shot…"

"The congressman's brand is misfortune, having a Canadian kill his niece." She made air quotes in the air. "It will be right on trend."

"Holy shit." He grabbed the top of his hair and let out a slow hiss. "But there were cameras all over the bar."

"Erased," she answered with little-to-no emotion, clicking away on her Android.

"And the cops?"

"Pretty sure they were bought and paid for. Those two dicks have the worst records on the force, and lo and behold, they catch the call." She snorted.

"DNA?"

"Safe, because you took her to the correct hospital. They specialize in battered women and rape. Don't worry. Detectives Hoyt and Alonzo won't be getting anywhere near her evidence to destroy it."

"Funny," he said, but didn't laugh at her reference to Andre's favorite movie, *Training Day*.

"The congressman has released a statement about the crime." Doris scanned her phone. "He promises to find whoever is responsible for his niece's attack." Doris chuckled. "Psychotic fuck stick."

"Hey, man" — Knox tapped the driver's seat — "take me back to the hospital."

"Keep driving," Doris demanded.

"Are you crazy? You know what the congressman is up to. Remy — "

"Right now is safer than you are."

The driver pulled the truck alongside his building. From what he could tell, the lobby had already filled up with press.

While they had been at the hospital, he had caught the breaking news that blared across every television screen. *The wife of the Mavericks' QB assaulted at a bar* had run across the ticker. There were no suspects yet, but the implication from the pictures posted that afternoon of Remy and his fight pointed toward him.

"There will be a specialist to work on your security and Internet," Doris explained.

"When can I see Remy?"

"Huh, good question." She finally glanced away from her phone. "I'll be in touch." He opened his mouth but knew this woman held his whole life in the palm of her hand. Knox got out of the vehicle and waited for his publicist to drive off.

Contemplating whether to go back for Remy, regardless of Doris' threat, Knox headed for his garage, with every intention of getting in his car.

"Hey," Mooch said. He stood near Hawk. Without a word to either one of them, he keyed in his code to open the door. The hockey player pushed off the wall and walked into the garage with him.

A slim chick with glasses stepped from around Remy's shiny truck. "Hi."

"Whoa." Mooch jumped.

"What the hell?" Hawk drew his fist back, ready to fight.

"Sorry," she chuckled. "I'm tech security…Daisy. Doris didn't tell you?"

"She said something about the Internet," Knox muttered.

"Yeah, I did that last week." She waved off his concerns.

"When?" Last week Knox had been at camp.

"Look… Can we talk in your place?" She rolled her hand in a wrap-it-up manner. "This building is crawling with paparazzi." Nobody moved. "Seriously, do you dudes want to frisk me?" Daisy held up her hands. "But I get to pick who does it."

"No," Knox said. "Let's go up."

"Are you sure?" Mooch asked. "We don't know her."

Without answering, Knox stepped into the elevator and everyone piled in after him.

"So are you guys some kind of boy band or something? I don't get out often."

"Uh, no. We're sports—"

"She's messing with you, dude," Hawk cut Mooch off.

Nervous energy slapped at Knox. It damn near suffocated him. Thankfully, the elevator stopped before he lost his shit in the tiny box. The doors opened to at least half a dozen women standing in his living room.

Knox could tell his grasp on reality had become tentative at best. A break had happened somewhere after their visit to the clinic and his wife's assault. Everything had flipped into a hazy blur that didn't completely register.

"We're Doris' little team of hackers, hired to get your wife back."

"What do you mean *back*?" Knox asked.

"Fuck me, Doris." Daisy dropped her head back with a groan.

"I told you she didn't tell him," one of the women said.

"All bark, no bite," another chimed in.

"Okay, there's no way you two can occupy the same condo, let alone the same country, with that maniac on the loose—"

No, no, no, no, no, his mind screamed. At the hospital, he had known this could happen, but not this soon — or hopefully ever. "She'll be put up somewhere until I can join her, right?"

"Dude, he tried to murder her and set you up for it."

That clawing feeling turned into an itchy, burning sensation that tried to prohibit easy breathing.

"Knox, man, are you okay?" Hawk asked.

"That's not what's happening right now. She got a nick. She should be out of surgery. Just call her. Remy's fine and she's coming home. Here... Let me go back to the hospital. Doris made me leave, but—"

"Sit down," Hawk roared. "Mooch, water. And you, Internet girl" — the big guy pointed at Daisy — "talk!"

"Doris made you leave because you're covered in your wife's blood and the press will have a field day with that image of the quarterback... Well, you know. Also, to keep you both alive, we have to keep you apart."

"What blood?" Knox found a free seat in front of his iMac. He didn't remember inviting people over. *Why are so many people in my house and where is Remy?*

"Damn it," Hawk said. "What do you mean *alive*?"

"The man trying to kill her is her uncle by marriage — and he's running for President."

"Are you fucking kidding me?" the hockey player growled.

"And we need Knox to tell us everything he knows about Remy. Just start from the beginning." The perky girl from the elevator sounded sad. It didn't matter. Once Remy got home, she would make them all leave and Knox could get his life back.

"Why?" Hawk asked. He sounded mad, which seemed about right, but Knox couldn't be too bothered with that. Instead, he wondered if he could talk to Remy.

"The congressman has tampered with evidence for years, and we're pretty sure we can find a spot he missed." The chick he hadn't invited into his home continued to babble. "We believe Remy has enough information. If we can access her storage online, we'll have a pretty good jumping-off point."

A group of people stared at him. *Expecting what?* Knox wondered where they had all come from. He didn't remember inviting any of them over. Before he could ask everyone to share their name, Hawk blocked his view with an open bottle of water.

"Drink this." He liked his water room temperature, but his wife needed hers close to freezing. "We need you to tell us stuff about Remy," his friend said.

"Ask her yourself. We're going to O'Hare in a minute."

Hawk leaned down until they were face-to-face. "We can't go get Remy until you tell us about you two. Now drink your water and start talking, okay?"

"Sure, but then we can go to the airport and pick her up, right?"

The big dude sighed. "Yeah, man." His smile seemed disingenuous and tight.

Something didn't sit right with him, but Knox nodded and chugged his water. They were best friends. *Why would Hawk lie?*

Chapter Twenty-Three

While most of the women plugged away on their laptops, a couple of them gave him their undivided attention.

Knox ran down for everyone how he had first met Remy.

"Here." Hawk passed him another bottle and took the empty out of his hand.

"Found a camera," someone said. The group mumbled indiscernible words that only they seemed to understand. Everyone typed faster on their keyboards.

"What camera?"

"Of the attack. We have a good visual. We're going to send a copy to Doris."

"What about the police?" Hawk asked.

Someone snorted.

"Uh, no. Doris will figure out which media outlet to send it to. They'll clear any doubt that has been placed on you and your friend," the only black woman in the room said.

"Here." Hawk threw him a shirt.

Why would I need this?

"Keep going," Daisy said.

"Do you really need it from the start? Shouldn't I jump around to—?"

"Where you left off. We need her passwords and would have had them by now, but she's..." Daisy looked around the room.

"I'm Bumblebee." The black woman chucked her finger at her chest. "Ah, your wife's a pro at running and she needed to be. I mean, for her to stay alive this long against a man who can make police reports disappear, she had to be on top of her shit."

Knox was still foggy about how he'd gotten back to his apartment and his mouth felt dry. "Give me a sec. Sorry." Heading for the guest bathroom, he stepped over the group of techies who took up every inch of his living room.

Flipping on the light, he took a step back from the mirror. Blood covered his tank and matted his hair "Shit." He turned on the water and stuck his head under the faucet to help drown the constant flashbacks of Remy's attack. He cleaned up and went back to reliving parts of his past on super speed. Knox walked back into the living room.

"Hey, big guy, remote."

Hawk looked confused for a moment before he picked it up from the table and tossed it to Daisy. She flicked on the TV, accessing the Internet for the top trending video. "Sorry," she apologized.

A camera shot the vantage point of the door outside of Jake's bar, Murphy's Pub. For the second time that night, he witnessed a man attack his wife. Knox headed toward the balcony door and opened it. He didn't need to see it again.

Still hot outside, he allowed the sticky air to cling to him. Leaning down, he rested his forehead against the balcony railing and beat back the urge to vomit.

"Your parents are on the phone," Hawk called.

Knox waved him off. He had barely averted a nervous breakdown earlier. If he talked to them, he would fall apart.

"Yeah, he'll call you back."

"The congressman will be landing at O'Hare Airport in less than an hour. We're going to need you to pick up where you left off," the bossy chick shouted. He stood up to walk back into his condo to relive the shit that at the moment hurt like hell.

Call it gut intuition, but Knox didn't trust Remy to actually show up for their date. Leaving his Nissan Coupe with the valet, he hoped she didn't stand him up. He'd never worked this hard for a girl in his life. Nerves shot through him in waves. Even a big game had never left him feeling this jittery.

Knox drew up short. "Whoa, Heartbreaker."

Remy stood in front of the restaurant. With her black curls piled on top of her head, the lines accentuated her high cheekbones, big eyes and slim neck. A strapless black dress hugged her every curve. God, he wanted to place his lips against that neck.

"Yay, I get a nickname," she cheered.

"I felt that was more appropriate than the other ones I've been calling you." He held open the door to the restaurant.

As she walked under his arm, she stopped directly in front of him and tilted her pretty heart-shaped face up to his. Invitation for a kiss? He doubted it. Knox didn't take the bait, but Lord knew he wanted to. "Like what?"

"We're not there yet," he repeated her words back to her.

Remy laughed hard. Placing his hand gently on her waist, he ushered her into the restaurant. They were seated quickly, which he hated. Every bit of time he had with her, he wanted to savor.

"So-o-ory." He stopped the hostess. "My legs are super petite. We're going to need a table for the height differential."

"Oh, sure." The hostess laughed at his joke. She changed gears and put them at an out-of-the-way table by the window instead of in a booth.

While he pulled out her seat, he got an eyeful of her cleavage. Knox hurried to sit down. Note to self, hard-ons are super apparent in khakis. "Looking at you, I feel underdressed."

"No worries. It's a cultural thing." Remy opened her menu and studied it.

"Hmm-m-m, I have a feeling you're calling me 'white boy' in your head right now."

"Not at all," she chuckled. "But you're not from here, are you?"

"What makes you think that?"

"So-o-ory," she repeated his apology from earlier.

He cringed in response. "Canadian. I can't shake that or ab-oot."

"And you're easy. I mean, your spirit is chill."

"Nah, I totally put out on the first date. Not that I'm skanky or anything, but I'm going to need at least thirty minutes." He checked his watch. "Or another hour anyway." Remy's laidback laugh helped to chip away at his nerves. "Give me a hint as to your full name?"

"Ah." She slid her hand along her collarbone and tilted her head to the side. Fuck! A completely innocent gesture forced him to drop his napkin on his pants for an excuse to adjust himself. Sexy radiated off her in waves. "It's something that you need but can never get enough of."

Knox ducked his head with a chuckle. "I totally deserved that."

Dinner went fast. On one hand it was a good thing – he had enjoyed her company – but bad that he had to let her go. "Check," he told the server.

"It's been taken care of." The waitress winked at Remy.

"But I…"

She put her soft hand on top of his big mitt. "It's the least I can do for giving you so much grief."

Knox didn't know what to feel. Annoyance crept into his spectrum of emotion. However, the sheer boldness of her gesture had come off hot as hell.

"Not that I don't appreciate you taking me out, but I did ask you for the date."

She shrugged. "Then you should definitely pay the next one."

Relief flooded his system. Thankfully, he wouldn't have to resort to begging, since he wasn't above it.

When they left the restaurant, Knox escorted her to the waiting Uber. He wanted to drive her home, but more than anything, he wanted her to be comfortable.

"Well, thank you for emasculating the shit out of me." He stood close to her. The scent of cinnamon and something similar to honeysuckle warmed his nose. Without accepting the warning that his brain sent to his heart, he dipped his head to capture those pretty lips that he craved. Remy leaned into his touch. Bearing in mind that Heartbreaker kept him rock hard with a mere glance, he reluctantly pulled away. "So-o-ory… Was that too forward?"

She smiled at him in that teasing manner he had come to enjoy. "It's just that I don't generally eat red meat," she said with a note of humor.

Knox had wolfed down a slab of beef at dinner – growing boy and all. He would have never imagined she would use his choice of nourishment against him.

"Uh…" He met her brown eyes with a penetrating stare. "You know how the Cookie Monster wrecks those cookies like nom, nom, nom, and Scooby Doo is like a fiend for his *snacks?" He nodded his head and waited for her to follow his thought process.*

"Yeah," she finally agreed, before she darted out her tongue and licked her bottom lip. Habit? *Nah, he didn't think so.* Cool-ass Heartbreaker might be turned on. *Finally, a point for him.*

"Well, I eat the shit out of meat," he whispered close to her lips. "I. Fuck. Meat. Up." He kissed her lips again — this time harder.

All eyes in the room were on Knox. "Did that nasty shit work?" Mooch asked.

"He had me at Cookie Monster," one of the hackers said. Light chuckles lifted the thick stress before heavy silence blanketed the room. A knock at the door interrupted them. Hawk left to answer it.

"Is she out of surgery yet?" he asked.

"I'll text Doris," Daisy told him.

"Hope you don't mind." A minute later the big guy came back with a stack of pizzas. "It looks like a long night ahead."

As Hawk passed around plates and boxes, the whole scene blew him back to the days of college all-nighters. Knox wandered toward the television. On the news, a static shot of Jake's bar flooded the screen, along with pictures of the disagreement he'd had with Remy from earlier. Closed caption explained the assault and the confusion around the mysterious assailant, inadvertently pointing the finger at him.

"These women are working on getting you off the hook, and once that happens, he would have gone after me, right?" Mooch joined him in front of the TV.

"A loose end is running around the city. He needs a sleight of hand to save his goon," Knox muttered.

"And I have a record. My DNA is on file," Mooch admitted. The kid's melancholy energy poured off him in waves. "Remy knew."

"She has fight or flight down to a science."

"Doris said she's in recovery." They turned toward Daisy, who read the update off her phone. "She'll be there for an hour, then they'll wheel her to a room."

"When I can see her?"

"Press is everywhere, but mainly they're all over this place." Daisy turned the channel to the security. The media had all the exits covered.

"But nobody's with her."

"She's not alone, Knox. Trust me," Daisy tried to assure him.

"*I'm* not with her," he said, harsher than he should have. "And that's what matters."

The woman pouted. "We still need the passwords, so whenever you're ready."

"But what about when she wakes up? Can we –"

"No, she'll have no access to any digital devices, and in the case of –"

"A leak or a mole in your organization," he finished for her.

Daisy nodded. "Once we move her, very few people will even know where she is." The techie took her spot back on the couch. Apparently, the legislative arm of the government held a smidge of power, but being potential president-elect put the psychotic nutter in a whole different league.

Chapter Twenty-Four

Already in the thick of summer practice, Knox had stayed on campus for the season. During holidays he would head back to Toronto, but for the most part, he lived in Michigan all year around.

Over the last two months, he'd seen Remy. He would have loved to say exclusively, but figured that might be only on his part. Knox seriously wondered about hers. They'd made out once or twice, but since they only hung out in public, it meant those sessions never went too far. Frustrated as hell, he didn't really know where they stood. Afraid for the first time in his life that he would be friend-zoned, he felt plain stupid.

"Hey there, slugger. Do you want to ice that black eye?" Hawk opened the freezer and tossed him a bag of frozen berries. After being stuck in a bad play, he'd twisted his ankle. To retaliate against his offensive lineman, he had returned the favor and knocked the shit out of him. Unfortunately, the asshole had swung back.

Coach had threatened to bench them if it ever happened again. "So, are you going to introduce me to this chick you're hitting people over or are you going to keep hiding her?"

"The other way around," he muttered. While he tried to balance the bag over his eye, Knox texted Remy that he would be late. Simply bananas over her, he got the feeling she was using him to merely pass the time. She held this strange edginess that he couldn't quite put his finger on.

"No shit? You're the dirty little ugmo. Now I really want to meet her." Hawk laughed.

I'll come 2 u.

Door's open.

"So-o-ory, I think she's a ghost professional, so-o-o..." On his good foot, he hopped his ass to the bathroom for a shower. "Leave the door unlocked on your way out." He whipped the frozen bag at Hawk, who snatched it before it hit him in the face.

"Dude, you seriously need to get some." Hawk didn't date. He had a weird rule he'd made in high school. Thankfully, Knox didn't have to worry about Remy running into the man who didn't understand the concept of a girlfriend.

Sore as hell, he stripped off his clothes and turned on the shower to jump in for a quick wash. Remy had only stopped by his place a couple of times to cut his drive in half, but she had never stayed long. Knox still didn't know where she lived. Nothing added up with her. Obviously, he should let the dream of Heartbreaker go.

"Knox!" she called from the living room. "I heard you got a booboo."

Stepping out of the stall, he wrapped a towel around his waist and opened the door. It being a typical college apartment, he could pretty much see the whole layout. There were two bedrooms and one bath. Remy stood with her back to him, unloading groceries onto the kitchen counter.

"It's the summer. How did word travel so fast? There's barely anyone here." Confused by the bags of food she was unpacking, he approached her.

"A girl knows a girl who knows a guy." She turned around and raised her eyebrow at him. The towel probably didn't cover all that much.

While she clearly judged his state of undress, he took stock of her. High ponytail meant girl next door, but curls down framing her face meant wild child wanted to play. Luckily, her hair was down. He took in the rest of her – tank, long flowy skirt… Hold on! No bra! What the absolute fuck?

"If your foot hurts, we can stay in tonight. There's a million things we can do."

Tired of the free-falling tornado of confusion that consumed him whenever he got in Heartbreaker's hemisphere, Knox released an aggravated sigh. "Unless it starts with my dick in your pussy, we've got to go out."

Vacant, no expression. Nothing. That's it. Hot girl who had fallen into his arms simply wasn't for him. He would sulk for a minute or two, even three, but then he would find a way to get over her. Everything in his life had been affected by Remy's unexpected appearance and he couldn't afford it. If he didn't want his ranking changed in the draft, he needed to gain a better perspective, and he couldn't do it with this flipping gorgeous distraction.

"Hmm-m." She bit her bottom lip and turned those big doe eyes to him. "Dick in my pussy was one through nine, so it'll probably get super freaky once we hit the double digits, right?" Whipping off the towel, he wanted her to be sure. "Well, damn… I know what you can do if the football thing doesn't work out."

"The jokes… Could you curb them for like a minute? I'm kind of naked here." Knox approached Heartbreaker.

"Who says I'm joking?"

He grabbed her under her arms and lifted her to his lips. She was light as a feather. He put everything he felt into their kiss. When she wrapped her legs around his waist, Knox groaned.

After that it turned into a grinding, filthy frenzy of lips, teeth and body parts. He yanked her tank over her head and thankfully he was right about the no bra. Remy's tits were perfect.

"God, you're so hot." After he'd sucked her nipple into his mouth, he barely managed to limp his way to the bedroom.

"Holy shit, the way you smell, so-o-o damn good all of the time," he said, between kisses to her breasts and neck. "Do-over."

"What?"

Knox dropped the beauty onto his comforter and took in his porn dream, splayed across his bed. "Full disclosure… I've wanted you from the minute I saw you." Knox's cock stood at fully erect and painful attention, but he knew he had to spit this out. "If I had known today you would finally let me touch you, I swear I would have jerked off in the shower. So this is going to be fucking fast and I'm going to need a do-over. Got it? This one doesn't count."

He expected her to get up from the bed — or the very least laugh. Instead, she tossed her head to the side and smiled. "Okay, Supastar… You get a do-over."

Knox pounced. Somehow, he had held out long enough to make her scream his name. Somehow, he didn't die in the middle of the hardest orgasm he'd ever had that nearly blinded him.

"What the hell was that?" Remy huffed, out of breath. She fell back against the bed.

Your future husband's dick. Get real acquainted with it. *Gathering her close, he rolled her body into his side. "My ticket to your full name." The rumble from her giggles tickled his ribs. She adjusted her hair to lay her head on his pec. God, she felt good.*

"Don't laugh?" She kissed a spot near his nipple, causing those intense flutters to tickle his insides. Seriously, he began to turn into a junior high school girl in her presence.

"Unlike how you callously laughed at my dick?"

"No, I was laughing at the poor beating my pussy was going to take. That thing is huge!"

"An-n-n-n-nd now I'm hard again." He kissed the side of her head.

"Give her a minute. She's recuperating."

Knox chuckled. "Quit stalling and tell me your whole name and social security number, in case you run."

"Why would I run?" She rolled on top of him, smashing her full breasts against his chest.

"That anxious energy that sprouts out of nowhere. When I'm on the field, I have to settle my nerves or risk making the wrong play. If I don't, then lights out, someone else gets your spot in the pros. I can tell you want to run."

The sun blasted through the slats of his blinds. Knox had never imagined Remy in his bed, let alone in the middle of the day. Perhaps after an expensive meal by candlelight... Truthfully, he'd never thought he would get this far with her. She set the bar high. On the other hand, maybe smacking the shit out of his teammates had provided him with awesome superpowers.

"Requiem... My name is Requiem."

"Baby, your hint was the thing you need but don't get enough of."

"Which is sleep!"

"Bullshit. Sex, sex and more sex. Ask any dude. I thought your name was Forny." Hard as hell again, he flipped Remy onto her back.

"Who names their child 'fornication'?" She laughed underneath him. Joining in with her humor, he came up with the brilliant idea of a naked comedy club, since she found him so damn funny with his clothes off.

"The same people who name their kid 'sleep'. And since you won't be getting any of that shit today, let's test your theory." As he worked his cock into her pussy, she sighed into his mouth.

* * * *

"Email, email!" the young one propped at the kitchen counter screamed. "I'm in. It's 0718Requiem1018."

The first number was his birthday, the second Remy's.

"Maybe if he'd told us her real name sooner."

"So-o-ory," he said, even though he felt he was the one owed an apology. The tortuous process had worn him out.

"Remy just set a new record. We're usually faster than this. Hey, it's the congressmen. Turn the TV up."

Knox's chest tightened at the sight of him. Raised to never hate anyone, he had a hard time channeling that emotion when it came to Brooks Richard. He sincerely wanted the man to drop dead.

"My niece is out of surgery and resting well." Doctors, nurses and staff from the congressman's team surrounded him. "We don't know who could have committed such a heinous attack, but the Chicago PD is working diligently to solve this crime."

"What about her husband, Quarterback Gavin Knox?" a reporter asked.

As the congressman leaned over, a staffer whispered in his ear before he returned to the microphones. "At this time, we don't have any information on him or where he's at. Now, if you'll excuse me, I need to check on my niece. She's alone at the moment and she'll need someone to be there when she wakes up."

Knox clenched his fists. He wanted to break something…anything, but mainly the congressman's entire body.

"We hear you're throwing your hat in the ring for President."

"If I can stop senseless crimes like this from happening, I will seriously consider it. Now, if you'll excuse me." While he was escorted into the hospital by security, reporters yelled questions at him. He waved solemnly and made his way into the ER.

"Ready for one more? From what I can tell, she has two cloud accounts, and nothing I'm running works," the pixie girl asked, probably jazzed by her first password crack.

"That's enough." Hawk held up his hand. "Really, look at him."

"No, I'm good. Let's do this."

"She's not even my wife and I'm having a hard time. Are you sure?" his best friend said.

Mooch nodded his head. "I've got to agree with Hawk. You need to take a break." The kid had kept quiet most of the night, either cleaning up after the hackers or grabbing them whatever they needed. Knox appreciated his help, but he probably couldn't properly convey that sentiment. For hours he had run on nothing but fumes.

"The longer this takes, the longer he can play the good guy." Knox wanted everyone to know about this insidious man.

Chapter Twenty-Five

They were headed to Cancun in a few weeks and Knox wanted to bail. Unavoidably, name-calling would occur – 'bitch-ass mofo', and familiar terms of endearment that questioned his manhood. Of course, the only hit that would be accurate was 'pussy whipped'.

The thought of leaving Remy for a drunken bender in Mexico had caused a ridiculous amount of anxiety inside him. He'd had girlfriends in the past, but football always took precedence. Knox had never given up bro-time for a chick. However, the one thing that he felt deep down in his soul was that Requiem Bell was a bona fide runner.

"So, is this girlfriend coming or what?"

Probably not, *he thought. While a mixture of football and hockey players fought over whose turn it was on the PlayStation, Hawk pawed one of his regular randoms. The hockey player had always been balls deep in a heavy rotation of girls since junior high school. Knox, on the other hand, usually kept his interactions to one at a time.*

"Not sure. Let me check."

He texted.

Where are u?

Remy had never made it to these impromptu get-togethers. She generally showed up once everyone had already left. If she did happen to make it, she would slip out before dawn. Knox was determined to pin her down, but it appeared Heartbreaker was a no-show. Again.

Outside…

Confused, Knox headed for the door.

"Hey, no ditching us for phantom girl." The big guy chuckled, already buzzed. Knox shook his head. Hawk had been diagnosed with type one diabetes years ago. No one on the team had a clue, but the hockey player knew better than to get drunk.

When he opened the door, steamy heat smacked him in the face. The parking lot was virtually empty. A handful of students had moved back to campus early, but the true rush wouldn't happen for another month. Eerie silence met him outside.

He texted.

Where?

As creepy-crawlies ran up his spine, he stepped out of the apartment. Hoping to knock off that foreboding feeling, he dug his hand in his pocket for his keys.

He focused on a crazy image in the far corner parking slot. Confused by what he saw, Knox broke into a light jog. "Remy," he called out. Not too far from the apartment entrance, she stumbled.

Reaching for his car, she missed and fell to the ground. Knox sprinted toward her and skidded to a stop.

"Who did this?" He knelt down in front of her. The dim glow from the streetlight showed her bloodied face. When he slipped his arms around her waist, Remy groaned from the touch. "What? What?"

"Ribs."

He lifted up her shirt. Her whole right side was covered in bruises. "Are they broken?"

"I don't know," she whimpered.

"Hospital... Let's get you to the hospital."

"No, no, no." As desperation shone in her beautiful eyes, tears slipped down her cheeks.

When he gathered her close, she moaned in pain. Placing her in the car, he felt helpless. "So-o-ory."

Keys, keys, keys. He forgot they were in his hand. Knox hurried to the driver side and got in. He couldn't think of what to do next. Shoving the key into the ignition, he started the car and backed out of the lot at top speed. Once he changed gears, he pointed his Nissan in the direction of the expressway and took the route to the only place he could think of.

"Call home," Knox told his Bluetooth.

"My boy," His dad answered right away. "Let me guess, you need beer money."

"Papa, j'ai des problème." Knox switched to French to tell his dad that he was in trouble.

* * * *

Everything had changed the minute he'd found Remy's battered body. His father had allowed Knox to call the family doctor, who confirmed she had a fractured rib, a busted lip and too many bruises to count.

Canceling his summer plans, he spent the next four weeks at his parents' farmhouse in Ontario. Soon his senior year *would begin. Knox didn't want to leave her, but there was no way Remy could return to campus.*

In eighteen months, his father would be up for reelection in his cabinet position. The old man had his eye on being Prime Minster of Canada. Knox knew he had a hard sell on his hands.

As they sat at the kitchen table, he fiddled with an empty bottle of water. The previous night his parents had flown to Ontario. He wanted them to get acquainted with Remy first, before he made his big pitch.

They sat opposite him. Mama provided a warm smile. Dad, on the other hand, sat pensively peering over the top of his glasses. "She's lovely and gorgeous." Mom whistled low with a chuckle.

Too nervous to do much more than puff out a heavy breath, he ripped the label off the bottle.

"This is the first time you've brought someone home to meet us, oui?*"*

*Remy's bruises were still apparent, but nothing could hide her beauty. "*Je veux la marier,*" he blurted out his intent to marry her.*

"You can't save her," Dad finally said, after what seemed like an eternity. "Marriage citizenship isn't guaranteed. She would have to live here for at least five years before she could qualify."

Destroying the plastic bottle in the palm of his hand, he tried to think of something that would make them see his point of view, but came up empty. The whole idea seemed crazy, even to him, but he loved her.

"It doesn't matter." Set on his decision, they couldn't change his mind.

"What about university, the pros, all your dreams?" Mom asked.

"Nothing's changed. I'll graduate then play football in the US."

"*Gavin, this is* fou, oui?*"

"*No, ma'am.*"

"*Hi.*" Remy *stepped into the kitchen.* "*Am I interrupting? I can go if…*" *The weird energy had probably slapped her in the face at the entryway.*

"*No.*" *He stood up, scraping his chair across the Spanish tiles.* "*We're done. Let's go for a walk?*"

As he met her at the back door, Remy gave him a tentative smile. "*Are you sure?*"

"Un tel spirit libre va vous écraser," *Mom said. The translation? Remy would crush his soul.*

Knox placed his hand on her back and hurried her out of the house. He didn't want them to switch to English. "C'est son coeur," *Dad replied that Knox could make his own decisions.*

They stepped outside and walked into the canola crops that grew in the back of the farmhouse. She wore one of his mother's white sun dresses. Her chocolate skin glowed in the midst of the yellow flowers.

"*How do you feel?*" *Knox touched her cheek where the worst bruise had been. To him, she was back to perfect, and he admired her beauty.*

Turning her head, she kissed his palm and smiled. "*Better.*"

"*And your ribs?*"

She let him go and began her trek again.

As he followed behind her, she ran her hand across the rapeseed. Two acres of yellow flowers that made canola oil, among other things, stretched for miles in front of them. "*We're not banging in this field if that's what you're asking.*" *Remy laughed.*

Rock hard, he rubbed his hand against the crotch of his jeans and tried not to focus on how hot she looked. "*Can't blame me for trying.*" *He sighed.* "*School starts next week.*"

"Yeah. I dropped out, so hopefully that will throw the asshole off my trail."

Knox ran his hand down her back. "Marry me?"

She stopped suddenly and turned toward him. "No."

"What? But it will help with citizenship and you can stay here in Canada, finish school here."

"That's…" Remy scrunched her face into a frown. It wasn't the reaction he had hoped for. "That's sweet, but I'll figure it out."

Shit, he couldn't admit how much he loved her. Never in his life had he experienced that deliriously happy, sweat-inducing feeling. "Not saving…helping. I'll go back, get my degree and play professional football. After five years, you get your citizenship. Maybe that psycho will lose interest or, at the very least, you'll be married to someone famous as hell."

Remy chuckled at that last part, which eased the tension in his chest. He sensed a smidgen of a chance.

"But you and your family have done so much already…" Turning away, she continued through the field.

"Being married to a diplomat's son allows you a certain amount of protection. He won't be able to touch you." A slight stutter in her step told him that he had her on the ropes. Knox hurried around to the front of her.

Adding his heartfelt plea for her to stay with him would one hundred percent guarantee a hard sprint in the opposite direction. He decided to appeal to her analytical side.

"We're not going to be together for long periods of time, and let's face it… Long distance doesn't work." While she tucked one of those wild and sexy curls behind her ear, she bit her lower lip.

"How about if I catch feelings for someone, I let you know in advance?" He gently put his hand around her waist to pull her close.

"Are you serious?" she asked.

"Hey, I'm the one putting it on the line here." Since he had no intention of loving anyone but her, Knox managed to say that mess with a straight face. *"We can get the marriage sealed, but it would look better if we didn't date other people."*

"And what if I'm interested in someone?" She spun away from his touch.

The thought had honestly never occurred to him. *"Just let me know,"* he replied, with every intention of ending that shit ASAP. *"Do we have a deal?"* The minute she provided him with a 'yes', his sole goal would be to knock her up. Interested in someone else? What the hell?

"D-e-a-l?" She drew out her words in the form of a question. Knox could tell she wasn't one hundred percent sure, but he would take it.

Lowering his head to peck those sexy lips, he inwardly rejoiced. He honestly hadn't thought she would agree. *"So, are you busy tomorrow?"*

* * * *

Knox fiddled with his phone, hoping Remy would text or call. The unknown was driving him crazy.

"Holy shit." One of the women had finally figured out the code to Remy's cloud account a few minutes before.

"Oh, I think I'm going to be sick," a different hacker said.

Not for the first time that day, his body seemed to work without much direction from his brain.

As the pixie chick vomited in his trash, everyone surrounded Bumblebee's screen. At six-foot-six, he rarely had to move anyone out of his way to see over them. When he joined Hawk in the back of the group, she flipped through crime scene photos, autopsy pictures and newspaper clippings of Remy's family.

Her parents had been shot in the head during a carjacking, while her aunt had allegedly hanged herself. Different evidence files and investigations were saved on her cloud account. In the far-off distance, someone cried.

His wife had hunted the congressman in the same manner he had hunted her.

Chapter Twenty-Six

Remy opened her eyes to a dim room and a dry throat. *What the hell happened?*

"Looking for that boy, aint'cha?"

She groaned at the sound of the congressman's voice. God, she hated him.

"He's down at the police station being interrogated. Hopefully they deport his Canadian ass. Even though he's a white foreigner, it will still look great on my record."

How the hell did he get in here? Remy scanned the room for a call button but didn't find one.

"Bo was never supposed to beat you that bad. I mean, back when you were at school."

She tried to scoot herself up but didn't have enough strength to move. Resigned to her fate, she lay there and listened to the ramblings of the sadistic asshole.

"He was supposed to rough you up enough for me to swoop in and save the day. Who knew you were with that idiot jock? I only caught wind of that shit after you ran. What was that, like the third or fourth time?" He chuckled. "Shit, you'd think you would learn that I will always find you."

Remy turned her head in his direction. He sat in the corner, shrouded in the darkness. Brooks had always been the perfect villain.

What the hell?

A normal life truly seemed too much to ask. She scanned the nearby table for a weapon.

"That looney aunt of yours had a head for numbers. Once she caught me siphoning money from her accounts, she filed for divorce. Who the hell did that gal think she was?"

Both sides of Remy's family had been fairly well off. Aunt Valentine, the creative sort, had flitted around from one endeavor to another. Mom had warned her younger sister about Brooks, but Valentine wouldn't listen.

"Your momma never believed her sister killed herself. She had the nerve to hire an investigator who petitioned for your aunt's remains to be exhumed. The only reason I didn't have that bitch cremated? Well, that sort of thing looks bad."

He was a charming, handsome devil of a man who had managed to snare her aunt into his web of deceit and lies. If she put aside his evil essence, Remy could understand Brooks' appeal.

The congressman stood up. Dark shadows played across his distinguished face. "The only thing I didn't see coming with that loon was her leaving all her money to you." He sucked his camera-ready teeth. "I've got to tell you that it was a blow. So I came up with an idea to kill your parents. That way I'd get *their* money, Valentine's money and *you*." He stood at the edge of her bed, inches away from her head. She willed her foot to his face — however, she couldn't feel her legs. The stuff in her IV was some seriously good shit.

"I didn't count on you being so smart." He wagged his finger at her. "You ran and stayed gone until you were old enough to collect all that money — depriving of me of my inheritance and that fresh pussy," he spat out, losing that charming tone he had perfected. "The thought of that big, football-playing doof wrecking what was mine just—" Brooks held his hand to his chest and took a couple of deep breaths, tapping a little beat. "Anyway, that's over, but let that little wound be a reminder." He shoved his face in front of hers. "You belong to *me*."

As he blew a bitter mix of alcohol and adrenaline in her face, Remy felt helpless.

"Congressman?" Completely mesmerized by his sheer closeness, she hadn't heard anyone come into the room. Several people crowded her doorway. "I don't believe you're on the list of visitors." Doris emerged from the group.

Brooks pulled away from Remy's face and hurried to cover his vicious essence with a bullshit smile. "I'm positive that has to be an oversight. After all, I am her only family." He patted the back of her hand.

Remy jerked away from his touch.

"No, sir. Her next of kin is her husband," Doris said.

"Who isn't here." He sneered.

"Mr. Knox is giving a detailed description of the man who stabbed his wife to the police."

Brooks snorted. "Are you sure that's not a smokescreen? Anyway, who are you?"

"Oh, sorry." Doris stepped into the room, along with several women the size of linebackers. "I'm your worst fucking nightmare. Now step away from my client."

The congressman clutched the bed frame before he gained his composure and chuckled. "What's with the hostility, sweetheart? Surely you don't believe I would do my niece any harm?" While he pleaded his innocence, he took a small step away from her.

"Yeah." Doris waved him off. "Save that shit for your idiot constituents. What you're going to do right now is go outside. Get in front of those cameras you love and tell the press how Gavin Knox is giving the police a description of the attacker. Throw in a little smile with a two-step for all I care, but convey to them that the quarterback is totally and utterly distraught."

Brooks chuckled. "Why would I do that? He could be shooting up with GHB or steroids as we speak."

"True, but the video surveillance that didn't mysteriously get erased like the other camera footage in the area shows a pretty beat-up assailant. He's running away from the scene. It would be helpful for you to make my client appear heartbroken." Doris stepped between the bed and the congressman. "Because if even a small kernel of evidence turns up implicating that your ass-backwards cousin had anything to do with this, I'll have it on every morning news show...ASAP."

For a shadow of a second, the congressman's face contorted into pure rage before he trained his expression back to normal. "Get better, hon." Brooks leaned over to kiss her cheek. "I'll be seeing you real soon." He straightened up and slowly strolled out of the room with the confidence of a man who would never get caught.

Doris whistled low. "Sorry, Remy." She held her stomach and took a deep breath. "They weren't supposed to let him into your room. I didn't know... Shit." With shaking hands, she pushed back her perfectly coiffed silver hair.

"Knox?" Remy asked.

"He's fine. We've got the techies with him." She patted Remy's hand before she clutched it really hard. "Shit. We're going to have to move you faster than we thought. Hang tight. We're getting you the fuck out of here. That sick son of a bitch pretty much announced his presidential candidacy on the hospital lawn. Shit!" For someone of Doris' caliber to unravel, Remy knew she was in deep trouble.

* * * *

After working well into the early morning hours, the tech team packed up. Knox watched the news. A close-up shot of the attacker filled the screen. He tried to remember anything about the guy that would help but he couldn't. Blinded by rage at the time, his mind had gone blank.

"The first year you were drafted..." Hawk said. Knox turned from the screen. "Your parents sent me to you for spring break, said you felt homesick and to make sure you stayed put. That's when she left Canada, wasn't it? I was a designated babysitter?"

Knox scratched the back of his head and chuckled. His parents had known he would take off the first chance he got. It would only make sense that they would send Hawk to keep an eye on him. "Yeah, she left power of attorney papers for me on her bed and instructions on what my parents should do with her stuff before she left. There was no word on where she was going."

"Now that I think about it, you were hella edgy. I just thought you were stressed over being a rookie in the league, but—"

"She didn't run," Bumblebee said. While most of the team had already left, the woman was still working on her computer. "There are anonymous emails threatening your parents' lives."

Knox crossed the room. Passing over her laptop to him, she stood up. "Hey, Daisy, you got a minute?" Bumblebee caught the other hacker at the door.

Hundreds of threatening emails, all from the same account, ascended by date. *Sicko6669*. Knox picked a couple to read. They all had a maniac bent to them.

He only looked away once as the hackers exploded into screams. "Lovers' quarrel?" Hawk asked. After they'd found Remy's cloud account, the tension in his condo had become unbearable. Not in the least bit concerned about those two, he shrugged.

"I'm staying over, so don't complain about it." The big guy patted him on the back and headed to the guest bedroom.

While the women continued to hiss at one another, Mooch waited in the hallway to drive a couple of the hackers home. Knox nodded his thanks before he returned his attention to the screen. He opened the folder that had his name on it. Amazed by all of the pictures of them together, he took his time flipping through the shots. In a world of his own, he didn't hear Bumblebee return.

Reaching over him, she enlarged one of the pictures.

Cast in a blue color, a naked Remy glanced over her shoulder, with the side of her round, upturned breast on display.

A perfect work of art.

"That one makes me want try out a new lifestyle," she admitted. "I hope you took that picture. Otherwise, this will be a different discussion."

"Paris a few years ago," he said. "I picked up her camera and caught her off guard. She made me promise to delete it."

"I totally see why you didn't." She took her laptop back. "Um, look... I need to apologize to you. We don't deal with men, and this could have been handled a lot better. Most of us volunteer our resources, but Daisy and I are paid. I'm the resident shrink, and I'm the one who made the decision to separate you two."

"Why?"

She packed her laptop into her case. "Remy allocated you as primary, which makes you our main client."

He shook his head. "Sorry... I'm not really following."

"We knew the congressman was coming to the hospital and that he would send dirty cops. The odds that he would cause a scene to get you arrested were extremely high. We couldn't risk your image..." She grabbed her phone and eyeglasses off his table before she let out a sigh. "I feel like we treated you unfairly. Our clients are usually wives of high-profile men who beat the shit out of them or commit sexual assault, and we have to deal with the effects of..." She wiped away a tear. "So, uh, Remy will be moved until we can sort through all the evidence. It will be sent to a big-time hacker and she'll tie up all the loose ends." Bumblebee hefted her bag onto her shoulder.

"The no-contact rule has been put in place because Brooks has a lot more access as president-elect," he automatically repeated Daisy's words from earlier. His phone rang for the millionth time that day. A number he didn't recognize popped onto the screen. As he was reaching to hit decline, she stopped him.

"Answer it." Before she let herself out of his condo, Knox accepted the call.

"Knox."

"Gavin," Remy said with a raspy voice, "I don't have long."

The use of his first name… It was a bad sign.

"Baby." He let out a ragged breath that felt like he had held it in since this whole thing had begun.

"We can't—" she started.

Knox hurried to the balcony and opened the door, since he always got the best reception there. "Stop," he growled. "I don't care what office that monster runs for, just…"

The brilliant rays of the sun rose over Lake Michigan. With so many thoughts colliding around his head at once, he leaned over the railing and decided to spill his guts.

"When I asked you to marry me, I was wrong to make it seem like a favor. It was the only way I could think of to get you to say 'yes'. I loved you then and I should have told you, even if it scared the shit out of you—or me, for that matter. It was arrogant as fuck to bring you home while this asshole is still on the loose, and I'm sorry."

"It's been years and he's not going to stop. He's never going to—"

Refusing to hear the words that would inevitability end them, he steamrolled right over her. "Remy, the amount of time I'm willing to wait for you is infinite."

"We're leaving. I need the phone," someone told her.

"Knox."

"Say it, baby. Tell me what I need to hear. Say it," he begged.

"Tag." Remy choked back a sob. "You're it." The line went dead.

Officially shredded from the inside out, he slid his back down the balcony door. He didn't know how long he sat like that, but the alert went off on his phone. Bumblebee had sent him the picture of Remy that he'd taken in Paris. Closing his eyes, he leaned his head against the balcony glass and prayed that he would wake up from this nightmare.

Chapter Twenty-Seven

The press had hounded him nonstop. Three weeks into Remy's absence, the front office wanted him to do a sit down with *60 Minutes* or *20/20*, anyone who would help shine a better light on what had happened. Knox had declined all offers.

Five weeks after the attack, the football season had begun with the usual fanfare. In his head, Knox pretended Remy was on assignment. Of course, it had to be some remote location since he couldn't call, text or FaceTime her.

He had done his best to keep it together. With two-and-a-half months down, he didn't have much longer to go. Unfortunately, the congressman's campaign had picked up steam. He'd referred to the attack on his niece once or twice in his speeches but had kept clear of implicating Knox again.

The minute that the playoffs were over, Knox would scour the ends of the Earth to find her.

For his last season, he wished he could say things were great. The division between the rookies who wanted more playing time and the veterans who knew how to get the job done was getting worse.

"How's the wife?" Doug shouted. The rookies joined him in a laugh. Physically worse off than ever, the linebacker looked like shit.

"You need to be asking why you're sitting on the bench." Andre stepped in line with Knox. They stood in the wings, waiting to run out on the field.

"Maybe if everyone wasn't so busy kissing your dried-up fucks' asses, we would get our playing time, showboat and wife killer," Doug growled.

He wished he had the energy to beat the shit out of Doug, but he didn't care enough to bother.

As the crowd roared, the team jogged onto the field. Knox's fans continued to show up for him. The press had reported that Remy's attack had to do with an obsessed stalker, which had helped him. Attendance at the games remained high.

The media still wanted to know details about her assault, but Doris had kept things under wraps. She'd spun the narrative to the press that his wife needed time to heal.

At the end of the fourth quarter, Knox knew they were a shoo-in for the playoffs. His stats might have seen better days, but he'd still held his own. One field goal up, the Mavericks were in possession, but he couldn't see Andre.

He palmed the ball and jogged backwards. Shifting to the right to get a better position, he heard the hit then felt it.

Lights out… Everything went to black.

* * * *

The team doc flashed a penlight in his eyes. After having been taken to the team's second locker room, Knox sat on a bench.

"Concussion," the doctor announced. "I need to talk to Bane. I'll be right back." He slipped out of the room before Knox could say anything.

"Fuck!" Andre hit the locker door with his fist.

Knocked unconscious for the first time in his career, he would be out for the next game. It was a recently implemented protocol, a mandatory light return.

"That's it!" Andre hollered.

Knox gestured for Mooch to block the door. The kid sighed and slid into the running back's path.

"I swear… If you don't move," Andre cursed.

"Look, man. I don't want to be on the receiving end of this, but the fucking bastards are trying to get both of you out," Mooch told him.

"He's right," Knox interjected. "If you beat the crap out of Doug, then the rookies will get the next few games and piss off the rest of the season."

"That druggie is mad that Lisa finally bought a clue and left his ass. You know he blames you." Andre turned and stalked the locker room. Mooch's face switched from his usual impassive frown to mild interest.

"Remy," he muttered. Bile worked its way up his throat. Knox fought to push it back down. His head hurt like a mutha.

"Did Lisa change her number?"

"Yeah, Lashonda told me she knew that dope fiend wouldn't leave her alone, so… Argh-h-h-h!" Andre punched the air.

"Mooch, go make sure Doug is gone," Knox said. He hated to make the only rookie he trusted do their grunt work, but if the jerk hung around, Andre would hand his ass to him.

"Are you out for good?" the running back asked. "This would be the perfect time to cut loose and find Remy. If it was my girl, I know I would."

"I wouldn't know where to start," he confessed.

"Shonda misses her. I know that doesn't mean shit, but…"

"No, it means something. Thanks," he told him. "So what happened on the field?"

"Our guys blocked your view, then Doug let the opposition whack the shit out of you. A linebacker on your left was about to snap your freaking spine, but Mooch got him. Trust me. That douche was seriously trying to hurt you."

"Now I owe the kid," he said, not completely surprised. Mooch had upped his game this past season.

"Hey, so while you're out on medical, stay with me and Shonda. Hawk is at an away game."

Knox raised his eyebrow.

"There's this thing called a phone. Damn, man. How hard did they hit you? I will never bitch down and say I watched hockey."

He laughed but stopped the minute every muscle in his body rebelled against him. Leaning to the side, Knox threw up.

Chapter Twenty-Eight

Nail guns, saws and numerous sounds that would drive a sane person crazy echoed throughout the cozy cottage. Ushered out of the United States in an amazingly swift fashion, Remy had been sent to an estate in Florence, Italy. Since the villa had been vacant for years, the roof had seen better days. A small team of locals was fixing it up.

Barely awake, Remy threw on a sleep shirt and went down to the kitchen. With coffee heavy on her mind, she stopped dead in her tracks at the sight of Claire Knox in the kitchen.

"*Chèri!*" Before Remy could back out of the doorway, Claire called to her. "I forgot how late you sleep. Sit."

Sighing, Remy took a seat at the café table. Holding two china cups, Claire stepped away from the stove.

As a politician's wife, Claire had learned to school her delicate features eons ago. Not the least bit fooled,

Remy could tell the woman was simmering with anger underneath her tightly controlled façade.

"Coffee?" Remy asked, but didn't hold out too much hope for the good stuff.

"*Non, thè de fleur. S'asseoir,*" Claire admonished her in French before setting a cup in front of her.

"The doctor said I didn't have to go cold turkey, and—"

Claire held up hand. "Tea. Now tell me, sweetheart. What the hell were you thinking?"

Buying herself some time, she picked up her cup and blew. The flowered leaves smelled divine but the drink didn't hold a candle to coffee.

"All these years…" Claire continued to reprimand her. "We've worked so hard at keeping you safe, then you lose your mind. Why did you go to the one place you weren't supposed to?"

She didn't have a good excuse. Settling on silence, Remy even contemplated tears, but she knew Knox's barracuda of a mother wouldn't fall for it. "Uh, well, Gavin asked…" she petered off, sounding ridiculous, even to herself.

"My son dug a stupid hole playing games with the tabloids and he needed to crawl out of it by himself." A cookie-cutter Stepford wife, Claire sat across from her, dressed from head to toe in Chanel. Her Auburn hair, which was perfectly coifed, held only a small amount of gray. Claire was distinguished and beautiful, and Remy figured that the vast majority of Canada's residents didn't have the foggiest idea that she was the true leader of their country.

Generally, her husband's mom held a sweet disposition. She'd never had to encounter the full weight of Claire's wrath. Remy sincerely regretted striking the match that had ignited it. For the past six years, they had worked together without Knox's knowledge. If Remy had stayed away from the US, they might have had enough evidence to finally nail the congressman.

"This is not only about you and Gavin's determination to act out some modern-day version of *Romeo and Juliet*."

While Remy giggled at the image, Claire glared at her. Considering she was officially sequestered to the Florence villa until further notice, Remy bit her lip to stifle her laughter.

"That villainous fuck can*not* obtain more power," she seethed and set down her tea. "Various meetings with world leaders have been held and we all agreed that this man will not be the next President of the United States. Everything we worked for… Dammit, Remy." She slammed her hand down, rattling the cups, before putting her fingers inches apart. "This was how close you were to dying and giving that man the one thing he should never be… The title of leader of the free world."

Too angry to feel guilty, Remy snapped back. "Next time I'll jump out of the way of the knife faster."

"Had you held up your end of the deal, you wouldn't have been stabbed at all."

Remy opened her mouth to disagree, but Claire was right. She had promised never to be in the same country as Brooks.

"Lucky for all of us, I was able to intercept you from that dreary publicist. She was hell-bent on shipping you to Lord-knew-where."

"Sorry," Remy said, sincerely this time. "I should have bailed in Barbados. I'm just…tired of the constant grind of staying three steps ahead of him. For five seconds, I wanted to be normal."

Claire tapped her well-manicured nails against the ceramic tile on the table and blew out a breath. "Normal is overrated. Ask my son. It's precisely the reason he had a temper tantrum when he found out his wife was far more popular than him."

"In his defense," Remy smirked at Claire's backhanded compliment, "we never told him what I was really up to. Come on. I'm one step away from being a spy for the Canadian government."

Since the prime minister's wife had the inside track on world events, she would often provide Remy with ideas on what country to hit next. Then, she would use a lot of Remy's work to push her own agenda to a world platform.

"Oh, I must have missed the part where America no longer has access to Google. How silly of me." The women shared a laugh for the first time that morning. "Gavin is focused and sweet, but that ego…" Claire threw up her hands. "This time he needs to stew in his own mess for longer than a quick minute. He is so spoiled, that one." Claire reached a hand for Remy to take. Hesitant, she frowned, certain the gesture was a trick.

"Before you two married, I told Knox you would crush his spirit. If you die, Requiem, it would shatter him into pieces." Relinquishing her reserve, she grasped Claire's hand. "We have an excellent hacker working on the congressman. I'm positive we're going to win this time. Now tell me" — she grinned — "how's my baby's baby?"

After the stabbing, Remy had found out she was pregnant. Although the first trimester was almost over, she still worried about another miscarriage. The doctor had assured her she had entered the safe zone.

"So far, so good," Remy admitted, hoping it would stay that way.

* * * *

Knox sat in a corner booth at Moe's, which was packed to the gills. It had taken him a while, but he'd finally gotten the appeal of the blues bar. The regulars were there for the bands, maybe the appetizers, and apparently nothing else.

Once his concussion ban had lifted, the Mavericks had gotten back to business and won their division. Up next were the playoffs. Shooting for an unheard-of third Mega Bowl win, he counted down the weeks until he could finally leave the country to find Remy.

Knox held up his phone. "Mama."

"It's beautiful," Mom cheered on FaceTime. "Are you sure she won't mind?" During his time off, he'd found Remy's football article on his iMac. Apparently, she had finished the piece before the attack.

"Papa said you used to pick them with Remy, so I trust you." He'd allowed her to choose the photos for the article.

"This story is *magnifique*," she told him. Remy had written about the pain of the game and what the players went through to achieve all those accolades on Sunday afternoons.

"It's good, *oui*? Have you heard from Requiem?" he asked her.

"Why would you ask me that?" Mama appeared genuinely confused, but he knew better. Anyone from the outside looking in would think his father ran the country, but nothing could have been further from the truth.

It honestly hurt too much to talk about, so he didn't wait for an answer. "I have to go, Mama. Email me what you pick." He waved Bumblebee, who had just entered the bar, over to his booth.

"*Je t'aime. Au revoir.*" She blew him a kiss and disconnected.

"This place?" Bumblebee opened her eyes wide and slid in next to him. "What the hell?"

"Charming, isn't it?"

"That's a word that doesn't apply here." She handed him a huge manila envelope. "Before we get started, can I ask you something?" She nodded toward the TV screens mounted on the wall.

One of the tabloid magazines was picking apart the quarterback scandal. Ever since they had made the playoffs, the networks had run that crap on a loop. Thankfully, Doris had gotten all the women in the magazines to come forward and confess that he had been completely faithful to his wife and it all had been for publicity, plain and simple.

"Sure." He took a swig from the mug of his guilty pleasure for the week—draft beer and a basket of wings. He had to hand it to Andre. These damn things were good.

"The other chicks… You did it for a reaction, but why?"

"Uh, crap." Rubbing the back of his head, Knox thought about blowing off her question. "Ego. I never took Remy's job seriously. Every now and then I would catch an article. 'A cute little hobby' was all I thought. I had no idea she was into such heavy shit. We never talked about it and I was too arrogant to look." He took another drink from his mug. "We had a few extra days around Christmas. Originally, I wasn't going to go to see her, but I found a charter and headed to Greece." He slid the basket of wings over to her. She smiled and took one. "Remy didn't expect me, and when I got there, a full-on riot was taking place. Borders were being closed, tanks pointed at kids… I was lucky to find her."

"Oh, I got it." She took a bite of the chicken. "This is good," she mumbled over the wing.

"What do you get?"

"If she's going to risk her life, why can't she do it with you?"

Knox snapped his fingers and pointed at her. "Bingo."

"Wow, that was seriously selfish."

"Thanks. And you can kindly stop eating my wings now." He pulled the basket out of her reach.

"Sorry," Bumblebee chuckled and nodded at the envelope. "In there, you will find everything that will land Congressman Richards in handcuffs." She reached for a napkin and wiped off her hands.

"Seriously?"

"The hacker we send all of our high-profile cases to found enough to put the man in jail. But between you and me" — she glanced around the room before leaning in close — "it's not about the money anymore. She signed power of attorney over to you years ago and let it be known. He's obsessed with her — and the only way he'll leave her alone is if he's dead or behind bars."

"But if he sets me up like he tried to do — "

Bumblebee shook her head. "He just wanted to stick it to you. How would he collect on her inheritance?

Nope." She sat back in her seat. "This is about beating him at his own game, plain and simple."

Knox opened the envelope. He thought the same thing but didn't want to confess it out loud. He really wanted to kill that man. "Now what?"

"This will need to get into the right hands, and most people are one greasy payoff away from hell." She shrugged. "Honestly, I don't know who you can trust with this type of information—but good luck."

Chapter Twenty-Nine

The hoopla covering the Mega Bowl seemed more exhausting than the actual event. Amped energy and massive ego had thickened the air. Knox leaned the back of his head against the locker door and zoned out to his music. He should have been more nostalgic about the whole thing, but he needed it to be over. Officially a private citizen after this, he couldn't wait to find Remy.

While he waited for the Q and A for presidential candidates to begin at the town hall, Knox popped out his ear buds. Navigating between jacked-up game energy and a calm space, he rolled his neck and stretched his arms.

"How's the ole noggin?" Doug chuckled with a batch of rookies across the locker room. Unable to stand on his own two feet, the fool needed lackeys. "Did you hear me, wife killer?" Though Doug was pushing a hard twenty-nine years old, Knox was amazed at the man's lack of maturity.

Doughy and out of shape, the linebacker didn't see it coming. Knox lunged across the room. Punching him with his left, he held his throat with his right arm and pushed him against the lockers.

The pudgier version of the Bob's Big Boy statue gasped for air. "Did you forget that I was ambidextrous, Doug? Or did you forget that my contract's up and the league can't do shit to me if I beat your ass? What? I can't hear you."

A ton of commotion behind him didn't pull his focus from the drugged-out idiot's face, which was turning a brilliant shade of red. "You know what *I* think you forgot?" Knox applied a little more pressure to the big idiot's neck. "That I'm not a five-foot-six-inch tiny woman you can beat up and control with your money. Was that what you forgot?" Knox itched to beat the shit out of him.

"Those roids have you stupid as hell. You couldn't knock me out yourself, so you used other players to do it." He breathed hot, angry breath in Doug's face. "You are weak as fuck and it oozes from your pores," he growled, shoving into his throat enough to hear him gurgle. The fat fucker's eyes began to water.

"That's enough, Knox."

Before he let him go, Knox muffed his face with his hand. Doug dropped to the floor.

"You mutha fucka!" Doug choked. Knox turned around to face a mess. Clothing, bags and chairs littered the floor. Veterans stood in the front of the rookies. "You're going to pay." Doug pulled himself upright but continued to sputter. "Carter, you saw that? You saw what he did?"

"See what?" Bane stood near the locker room entrance.

"But you just—"

"Let's go, Renner. Time for a drug test."

"*What*? I already took one." Crazy red blotches appeared on his chest and inched up Doug's neck.

"Yep, and now you're going do another one," Bane told him.

"No way... You can't do this to me... You can't!" The test administrator stood outside the room, along with two guards. "I'm not doing it. Forget that shit."

The league officials had finally found the inside guy who had provided Doug with the drug test warnings. The heads-up had always allowed the idiot enough time to flush his system.

"Then you don't play."

The guards walked in and Doug slammed himself against the locker in some pathetic attempt at a childish fit.

"The show's over," Andre said. The rookies were the first to wander off, with a lot less enthusiasm. None of them were playing that night, and the veterans had decided to send them a message for the future.

As a strange silence filled the room, Knox's phone buzzed.

"Okay, everyone hit the hallway. Give us ten," Bane told him.

Andre grabbed Mooch by the shoulder and turned him around. "Not you, kid."

"Oh!" he said, surprised. They all had Google alerts attached to the congressman. Since they were in Florida for the Mega Bowl, they couldn't pull the feed for the Texas town hall that was being aired on TV. Pandering to his base, Congressman Richard had done a ridiculous amount of campaigning in the red states. His poll numbers were sky high.

"The next question is from…" the moderator who sat nearest to the candidates read off his cards. "This one is from the *Will County Gazette* in Illinois."

"Congressman…" Art stood up. "We have reports that show funds from your campaign contributions were used to pay for office furniture, trips and it says 'leisure', but the footage I have here…" As Art peered over his glasses in that patronizing manner Knox hated, he held up his tablet. Sounds of copious amounts of sex filtered through the sound system.

"Uh, we'll be taking a commercial break, and when we come back—" Someone tried to wrestle the microphone away from Art, to no avail.

"No, you'll want to stick around for this. Trust me. Congressman, those ladies were paid from previous campaign contributions to entertain Russian diplomats."

"Are we taking this clown seriously?" Brooks screamed.

"What's with the name calling?" Art pouted. "I'm simply asking questions about your record. It appears your votes consistently back a foreign agenda." Guards stormed from the audience, headed straight for the reporter. "You don't want to answer that?" Art held tight to the microphone and danced out of reach of security. "Those were the easy ones."

The guards roughly grabbed his arms before he could rattle off another question.

"We'll be back after this." The moderator smiled tightly at the camera.

"Now what?" Mooch asked, confused. "Nothing happened."

"Besides Art probably getting his ass beat outside that town hall meeting." Andre laughed, which kicked everyone off into a peal of giggles.

"The FBI is waiting to talk to the congressman, so they won't rough up Art too bad." Knox turned off his phone.

"Are you ready to win this shit and go get your girl?" Andre put out his hand. Knox slapped his palm and they both threw back their heads and howled.

Chapter Thirty

The Mavericks won the Mega Bowl and had pushed up their sponsored trip that usually happened a week later. Management wanted to fly Remy into Florida the day prior to surprise her quarterback husband. The only hitch in the plan was the congressman. He had placed her on a travel ban, which made it a freaking nightmare to get her back into the country. She had made it precisely thirty minutes after the parade in front of Cinderella's Castle.

Two very stern security guards had picked Remy up from the airport and driven her to the 'Happiest Place on Earth'. Since they couldn't even project mild amusement, she wasn't sure she'd gotten into the correct vehicle.

"So, what are you guys doing later?" She poked her head in between the front seats. "I hear Harry Potter's world is a must see. No, no…nothing?" Amped on pregnancy hormones and adrenaline, she tried to engage them in conversation. They drove the van into the backstage area of a huge theatre and parked it.

The team had a scheduled Q and A with the fans. When they finished all their Maverick duties — which included talk shows and club appearances — they could officially begin their off-season activities.

Someone slid the passenger door open. "Where the hell have you been?" Dahl yelled.

"Hi to you, too," she hollered back.

"Sorry, sorry." Dahl rushed her out of the van. Dressed in a sexy pink dress, the Mavericks' owner held out her hand to help. At four months pregnant, Remy had a bit of a bump. It wasn't that noticeable. However, the hormones and lack of caffeine were making her a straight psycho.

As Bane held the theater doors open for them, the roar from the fans flowed outside. Dahl placed a hand on the small of her back and hurried her along.

"Remy…" He nodded with a slip of a smile on his fierce face.

"Bane Carter, to what do I owe the pleasure of having two owners escorting me?" They power-walked through the backstage area.

"Apparently my quarterback's wife is on a terror watch list. Under threats of bodily harm and prosecutorial punishment, we promised park management that we would keep our eyes on you at all times."

"Welcome to my world," she said with a grin. Of course the congressman had to keep the surprises coming, even with all his legal troubles.

They rounded the corner to the standing-room-only theatre. The crowd waited for the players to get situated on the stage. First the press would have a crack at the team, then the floor would open to a select number of fans who were allowed to ask questions.

"This wasn't easy to pull off. We had to threaten Knox with breach of contract and loss of any future income if he didn't stay put for this."

Remy knew the second Knox could search for her, he would. It was a game they had played for years. A small part of her wanted to continue the chase, but they had to grow up. No more tag — the game was over.

"What happened to Doug Renner? The rumor is he didn't pass his drug test," a reporter asked the players. Knox sat at the end of the table, clearly not engaged.

While their small group moved within the shadows of the theatre, all eyes were on the Mavericks. No one paid the least bit of attention to them.

"Right before we hit the field for the Mega Bowl, Doug got pulled into a random drug screening," Jake said.

"That isn't usual, is it? Right before a big game?"

"I think that's why they call them random," Andre responded.

As the crowd clapped wildly at his smart comment, they hurried over to the wives' area. Lashonda stood in the aisle and waved her in.

"When you get a second" — Bane grabbed her arm to stop her — "I need to talk to you about something."

"What?" Remy turned around to face him.

"It can wait until later." Clearly uncomfortable, the big man glanced away.

"Hey, no prob. I mean, I've been on the run for a couple of years from a maniac who has had me beat up, hit by a car and stabbed, but please, let's talk about *your* thing."

"Oh shit." His face fell. "I didn't mean to imply…"

Dahl bit her quivering lower lip and Remy smiled. "Messing with you, big guy." She walked backward up the aisle. "Don't worry. I've got you." Dahl slipped her arm around her husband's waist.

"But you don't know what I wanted to talk to you about," Bane said. He still seemed unsure of himself.

"Sure I do." Remy hurried up the aisle to Lashonda.

"What took you so long?" she asked, before she took a hold of Remy's arm.

"I'm great, girl. Thanks for asking." Lashonda shoved her behind the other wives. "Where's Allison? I owe her something."

"Yes, you do," Lashonda agreed, "but you're going to have to give it to her some other time. She's not allowed to sit with us anymore." They laughed, while the press continued to ask their questions.

"This is the last game for the quarterback. How does it feel?" a reporter fired off.

"Knox? Hey, man…" Andre elbowed him. He turned his attention away from his phone and toward the crowd.

"What will you do after football?"

"I'm weighing my options," he muttered.

"The rumor is you'll work in the front office."

"Not sure yet," he said.

"How do you think you'll be as a new father?" a voice called out.

As the hall went completely silent, Knox stood. One of the rookie's wives had asked the question. They knew he wouldn't recognize her voice.

"Repeat the question?" The microphone went back and forth between the women until it finally got to Remy.

"As a first-time father," she said, "how do you think you'll do?" Remy stood in the middle of the wives, who picked up a sign from the ground that spelled out *Congratulations*. The sea of women parted.

"No shit?" he screamed once he saw her. A gasp rippled through the crowd.

"Whoa, man, this is a family show."

"We're on a delay, right?" a guy with a clipboard by the camera asked.

Knox hopped over the table and down the stage, knocking a couple of people over to get to her. "So-o-orree," he apologized as he ran.

"So-o-orree," the football wives screamed back.

He jogged down the aisle toward her. As he got close, Remy flipped open her sweater to show her dress that read *Knox's baby* on the front. He clearly took in the small bump that stood out. Gathering her into his arms, she immediately warmed to his touch. "Camp?" he asked, ecstatic. "Best twenty-five thousand dollars I've ever spent."

"I won?" she asked about the bet they'd made.

"No, I did," he told her. While the crowd cheered, he pulled her to him. "But what about your IUD?"

Remy rolled her eyes.

"Come on," he pushed.

"Displaced," she mumbled.

"So, I knocked that shit out. My super sperm knocked it out… Say it."

"So-o confident." Remy laughed.

She breathed in the heady scent of sandalwood and spicy leather.

"God, I missed you," he growled into her ear before he kissed her again.

"What's next, Supastar?"

Placing a hand on her small bump, Knox replied, "Everything."

Epilogue

She was six months pregnant and nothing in Remy's closet fit. They were shooting a documentary about the Mavericks' epic run and she had held up production to find something to wear. Lashonda had tried to style her but that had gone super south about ten minutes prior.

Almost a half hour after her call time, they had finally decided to rip apart one of Knox's shirts. Twenty minutes later, she walked into the studio. "Art." Remy hugged the old coot, who was also participating in the special.

"Why did you let him knock you up? We would have been so good together."

Dressed in his best tweed suit from the sixties, Art tried to keep a straight face and Remy laughed. "You're such a dirty old man. Thanks for saving me." Art had taken the file the hackers had compiled and he'd contacted some people he knew in the CIA and FBI. They had devised a solid plan to arrest the congressman, but only after Art got to confront him on national television. Brooks faced numerous charges, with embezzlement and treason at the top of the list.

"Nah, you saved *me*," the reporter said. "My career and dinky paper have never seen it better." Remy kissed the side of his cheek. "Let me know when you want to get rid of him."

Remy glanced over at Knox, who sat in front of the big television lights and camera, glaring at them. "You'll be the first to know." She smiled.

"Get the hell away from my wife, Artie!"

The old man chuckled. "What the hell do you see in that Canadian idiot?"

Remy made her way toward the camera. "Do we have to go over this again?"

"Nope, you win," he yelled at her back, while an assistant guided her over the cables in the studio. Knox took her hand to help her the rest of the way. Considering she was all boobs, she smothered him on her way past.

"So-o-o-o, what happened to that dress you packed?"

"Not now, Knox." She put up her face up for Lashonda to fix her makeup under the lights after she took her seat.

"Her tits are too big. That's why we needed to borrow your shirt."

"Shonda," she hissed.

"What? It's the truth? Look at them."

"Yeah, I told her yesterday that the dress she brought wasn't going to fit," Knox said matter-of-factly.

"But regardless of you two tearing up my shirt, you look fucking fantastic." He leaned in to kiss her.

"Don't forget. You owe me twenty-five thousand dollars," she told him, not bothering to mess up her makeup to entertain his patronizing crap.

"That wasn't the bet, baby. The bet was if my fine was—"

"Jilly!" Remy cut Knox's bullshit off to scream at the former intern. The girl made her way over to the producer's chair. "What the hell?" Remy was stymied.

"Hot Husband here got me the gig."

"So you should definitely forgive me for everything." Knox granted her a throaty chuckle and squeezed her thigh.

Pregnancy hormones had her annoyed with his presence in general. Nevertheless, Remy couldn't pass up hot sex. No one had told her pregnancy made women horny as hell. Of course, she would forgive him before too long. That was how it always happened.

"We just have to go through a couple of preliminary questions," Jill explained. Remy pointed at the camera. "It's rolling, but we're not going to use it."

Having never been interviewed before, Remy's nerves rattled her insides. As the intern got situated in the seat across from them, Remy tried to calm down. "When you two first met, was it love at first sight?"

"Uh, that's a weird question." Remy glanced over at Knox, but he offered her no assistance. Not used to interviews from the other side of the camera, she figured the truth wouldn't hurt... They couldn't use it anyway. "It was sweatpants season."

A roar of laughter went up.

"Got to pay for dinner, man." Knox pointed at Andre. "And White Castle is not on the menu."

"Sweatpants season is not the same," Andre hollered back.

"That was your 'mask-off' question," Lashonda told her while she applied more blush to her cheeks. "All the wives get one. The husbands pick something you may or may not tell the truth about."

"What was Knox's answer?"

"He told us you would say the closest thing to '*what does that dick do?*' in response to love at first sight," Jill read off her card.

Remy chuckled. "Sure, I thought that. I mean, he was wearing khakis on our first date, but I could still make out his hard-on—"

"Told you," Knox cut her off to taunt Andre. "And TMI, babe."

The group had plans to go out and eat later. Knox wouldn't let Andre get out of paying. *Rich cheapo*, she groused in her head.

"That shit's *not* the same," Andre muttered.

"Knox," Jill pulled his attention back to her, "do you want your son to be like you?"

"No." He snorted. "I'd rather he be like my dad— and if it's a girl, I want her to be a bad-ass like Remy or my mom."

"Ni-i-ice." Remy put her fist out for him to bump.

"Now, am I forgiven?"

"We're getting warmer."

Lashonda teased Remy's hair over her shoulder. Little braids were interwoven with her curls and the effect couldn't have been more adorable. Once she finished, the stylist stepped out of the way, allowing the lights surrounding them to hit her head on.

"Wow." She sat back. The full force of brightness stunned her for a second.

"Remy, what do you expect is the next step in Knox's career?" Jill rattled off another question.

"Mr. Mom," Knox interjected then chuckled. "Ever since she's been home, I haven't given her a moment to breathe. I think she's finally getting tired of me."

Knox had an amazing amount of pent-up energy. She could tell he didn't know what to do with himself. "He's still in top form, and right now, a fourth Mega Bowl with his longtime friend and running back would be his to win. Can you imagine him doing that for the first time in front of his wife and kid? I mean, it would be epic."

"Wait... What?" he asked, staring in awe. No smart remark graced his lips for the first time that day.

"Come on, man." Andre stepped over, holding up his phone. Bane's big mug filled the screen.

"Say the word," the owner offered, "and we'll draw up that contract."

Knox glanced between Andre and Bane before he settled on her.

"Come on, Supastar," Remy said. "You think you got one more in you?"

Knox's lips curled at the corners into the biggest brightest smile. "What the hell? One more for both of my babies."

Reaching out to slap hands with Knox, Andre howled before he turned to the camera. "I hope you got that shit on tape, because we're back and we're going to take it all."

"Requiem Bell, you are a warrior." Knox leaned in close with a lewd grin. "You're a gladiator. You're a beautiful beast." He closed the inches between them to peck her freshly-painted, glossy lips. "And I'm so happy I tricked you into marrying me."

Want to see more from this author? Here's a taster for you to enjoy!

Kill Shot
Amber Malloy

Excerpt

O'Brien's, the Midtown Manhattan pub, aired the NBA playoffs on every television in the bar. Walker Knight ordered another round of Jameson for his boys. His crew—younger than him by at least ten years—congratulated each other on a job well done.

"To the best security team this side of the Pacific." He lifted his drink for a toast.

"Come on, boss. We thought you were going to say 'in the world'," a newbie joked.

"That's a tall order. It'll take more than one job together for that." Walker wanted to celebrate, just not to the level of wasted. His crew had no problem staying up all night, but he needed to catch some zzzs. "Next round's on me."

They'd spent eighteen hours on a plane to the Middle East. In three short days the team had taken down a faction of a religious sect named Glory's Soldiers. Pleased with their quick extermination of the zealots, WLK Security's oil clients had provided them with a major bonus.

As he was signaling for the bartender to settle their tab, a newbie squeezed in beside him.

"What's next?" the rookie asked.

With a total of three partners—two from his school days and one silent—they ran a private security firm. Walker led their missions and could always tell the adrenaline junkies from the dedicated worker bees.

"Give it a couple of days," he lied. Walker honestly didn't think he would see the guy again. The kid's jumpy nature grated on his nerves.

The bar cheered at the Knicks' three-point basket at the buzzer. After signing the credit receipt, he chucked deuces to his crew. Dead on his feet, Walker headed for the exit. He couldn't wait for his head to hit the pillow.

As his phone vibrated in his pants, he fought the urge to ignore it, but habit forced him to fish it out of his pocket.

"Walker," he answered.

"Well, if it isn't my Knight in shining armor," the woman cooed.

Walker stopped in his tracks. That voice was straight out of his past. A form of Neverland—not all bad, but not one he wanted to deal with.

A shoulder check from a drunk blonde got him back into gear. She winked on her way past, and he smiled in return but offered nothing more. "Thought I would never hear from you again. How did you crawl your way back from the dead, Eden Morgan?" he said.

"Trust me. Raising twins is much harder."

Walker chuckled at the spy. J8, the American Intelligence Agency recognized as top in their field, had put her out to pasture by burning her status. Thankfully, Walker had never had to deal with the aftermath of her departure because he'd left long before that had happened.

"Since I'm positive this is not a social ring-a-ding-ding..." He pushed opened the door to the bar.

Shielding his eyes from the descending rays of the sun, he headed to his Jeep. "What's up?"

"I'm calling in a favor."

Walker searched around for the women on the other end of the call. Spies were the sneakiest devils. However, the busy streets gave no clue if she was in the vicinity or not.

"Sorry, sweetie, I got out of the game a long time ago."

"Don't worry," Eden told him. "No heavy lifting on your part."

He snatched open his Jeep's door to hop in. "There's nothing in me that believes that."

"We've been monitoring two lawyers from a good distance but one of them has gone off the radar."

"And you want me to find them?" he asked. Walker put the key in the ignition and waited to see what she would say before he started the truck.

"No, I'm pretty sure she's dead. We need you to intercept her partner and keep her safe until we can extract her. I'll send you the info."

"Hold up, Eden. I didn't agree to anything."

"That's the funny thing about favors, Knight. They have no expiration date."

As the text alert vibrated in his ear, she hung up before he could protest. He pulled his phone down to check the screen. The name E.A. Marcille and a location pin appeared. Nevertheless, Walker's interest didn't pique until he saw the profile picture accompanying the directions.

Why would anyone want to kill her?

Putting his truck in gear, he ditched his original plans and decided to go see about a lawyer.

Home of Erotic Romance

Sign up for our newsletter and find out about all our romance book releases, eBook sales and promotions, sneak peeks and FREE romance books!

About the Author

Amber Malloy dreamed of being a double agent but couldn't pass the psyche evaluation. Crushed by despair that she couldn't legally shoot things, Amber pursued her second career choice as pastry chef. When she's not writing or whipping up a mean Snickers Cheesecake, she occasionally spies on her sommelier. Amber is convinced he's faking his French accent.

Amber loves to hear from readers. You can find her contact information, website details and author profile page at https://www.totallybound.com

www.ingramcontent.com/pod-product-compliance
Lightning Source LLC
Chambersburg PA
CBHW030144180626
46812CB00002B/843